Sweet On You

The Wilde Sisters, Book 1

Marianne Rice

Sweet on You

Copyright © 2015 by Marianne Rice.
All rights reserved.
First Print Edition: January 2016

Limitless Publishing, LLC
Kailua, HI 96734
www.limitlesspublishing.com

Formatting: Limitless Publishing

ISBN-13: 978-1-68058-469-1
ISBN-10: 1-68058-469-3

No part of this book may be reproduced, scanned, or distributed in any printed or electronic form without permission. Please do not participate in or encourage piracy of copyrighted materials in violation of the author's rights. Thank you for respecting the hard work of this author.

This is a work of fiction. Names, characters, places, and incidents either are the product of the author's imagination or are used fictitiously, and any resemblance to locales, events, business establishments, or actual persons—living or dead—is entirely coincidental.

Dedication

For my baby sister. You'll always be the youngest and I'll always be the middle, and I wouldn't have it any other way. Smooches.

Chapter One

Trent

"There's no way in hell I'm making good on this freakin' bet." Trent Kipson glared at his best friend over the rim of his glass and chugged the rest of his beer.

"Dude. You lost. Man up. Pay up." His best friend Brian Smart, who he'd been making ridiculous bets with for the past twenty years, laughed and tilted his glass back.

"Seriously, Bri. This has to be the dumbest bet you've ever come up with. Consider yourself disowned." Trent signaled the bartender, who immediately filled another mug with Guinness and slid it across the bar.

"You're the idiot who agreed to it. I told you you'd be hit on before you finished your first beer. It's not my fault you're—" A blonde college girl with mountains of perky boob busting out of her low-cut shirt sidled in between them, interrupting Brian.

"Hey, aren't you that guy? Like the Cake Boss or something?"

Trent scowled at Brian. Now would be the perfect time to strangle his brother-in-law.

"No." He gritted his teeth and pried his eyes from the cavern of cleavage she flaunted.

"Yeah, you are. My roommates and I saw you on TV last week. You're even cuter in person," she drawled, running her nails down his arm. "Care to come on over to our table? Next round's on me."

He never thought he'd grow tired of the song and dance of a woman hitting on him, but the past month had tried his patience.

Brian snorted, making Trent regret coaxing him into a guys' night out. Ever since his fifteen minutes of fame last month, Trent had been inundated at the bakery. Who knew that a quick write-up in a paper and a mug shot of him decorating a celebrity wedding cake would go viral? The world was a strange place. Between the articles in *Yankee* and a few other high-end magazines in the New England area, and the airtime on the local news channels, he hadn't had much time for hanging out with the guys—or girls.

At first Trent was uncomfortable being in the spotlight, but when a producer from the Cooking Network contacted him last week about a possible job in California, he'd nearly fallen into the third tier of the McKennys' wedding cake. He'd be able to pay off his sister's medical school bills and crawl out from his own debt.

Social media had its perks.

"Whatdayasay?" The blonde stroked his cheek

with one of her long talons, bringing him back to the present.

"Um, sorry. I've got plans tonight." He smiled and turned on his barstool to face the rows of liquor bottles behind the bar, signaling his disinterest. The girl huffed and marched off.

"I take back what I said last night about you and the ladies. You haven't a clue."

"I'm glad you're having so much fun with my fifteen minutes of fame, Bri."

"I hear your name's trending on Twitter."

"Shut the hell up and finish your beer. The game's starting soon."

"Wanna make another bet on how long it will take for another desperate publicity-seeker to hit on you at the stadium? Let's see…the blonde was the third in…" Brian checked his watch. "…the twenty minutes we've been here. I wager you won't make it to the opening pitch before some chick recognizes you."

"Forget it, wiseass. No more bets."

"Don't be such a sore loser. I didn't cry last week when I had to hose down the fire truck in my boxers."

Trent rolled his eyes. "I beat you to the top of the mountain because you're a pansy ass. It's not my fault you were stupid enough to challenge me while breaking in a new pair of hiking boots. I, however, had no control over this bet. I can't help it if the ladies love me." He grinned.

"Ah, you're paying up, Kipson. I'm gonna *love* watching this one," Brian said, slapping down a few bills on the bar.

No, Trent would not allow Brian to watch him pay his dues. It was going to be embarrassing enough as it was. God help him.

***

Rayne

Rayne Wilde cranked up the music and tightened the elastic that held her thick, long hair off her neck. Ever since opening *In Motion* two years ago, her life had been a constant whirlwind of accounting, decorating, and choreography. Her early morning workouts were the few hours during the day when she could ignore the business side of owning her own fitness studio and do what she enjoyed: socializing and exercising.

Gleaming hardwood floors, enormous windows, rows of mirrors on brightly painted walls, and themed workout rooms made the studio fun, fresh, and hip. The Zumba room was her favorite. Zebra prints hung on a bright pink wall while three paler pink walls were decked out with inspirational sayings. Nothing calming in this room. Save that for yoga and Pilates.

Running her own business entailed so much paperwork and organizing, and thankfully her older sister, Sage, had good business sense and helped her with the spreadsheets and taxes. Her younger sister, Thyme, taught kickboxing and filled in at the front desk when Rayne was in a jam.

Her sisters rocked. And hopefully someday soon Rayne would have her own little family to dote on, to love and play with. Something she and her sisters grew up without. She may be only twenty-eight, but if she wanted a huge family, she needed to find the right man, Mr. Perfect, her soul mate.

Neil and Suzie Wilde never intended to have children, their *mistakes* happening when they were in their late thirties and early forties and already too invested in their own life to sacrifice anything for their three daughters. Rayne had been playing house and looking to settle down since she graduated from high school. Hopefully the man of her dreams would walk into her life soon and make all her fantasies come true. As if.

The six a.m. class filled up quickly. Monday mornings were typically the smallest class, but Tuesday through Saturday made up for the slower day. This Tuesday was no different. She hummed and wiggled as she went through the playlist for the class. Last week the girls were complaining about bathing suit season coming full-force this year. It was only early June, and Maine had been hit with three major heat waves already.

Pleased with her playlist and the two new songs and routines she worked on over the weekend, Rayne connected her iPod to the surround sound and Beyoncé echoed off the walls. Soon the room filled with tired moms, college girls home for the summer, and a few thirty-somethings still searching for Mr. Wonderful. Just like her.

"'Kay ladies, you ready to burn some love handles? Tighten those butts? Rock those abs?" Rayne shouted above the music. "Let's get our groove on! I've mixed some old with the new.

We'll start with our familiar stretching, though. Let's move!" She clapped her hands and turned to face the mirrors so the twenty-four women could copy her motions. They danced to Taylor Swift and bounced and boxed to Rihanna before she allowed them a quick water break.

While the class gathered their breath, she stayed in front of the mirrored wall and gyrated her hips. "All right, girls. It's booty time." Rayne pulled in her belly button and swirled her hips to the left and then to the right. "This next routine is new. I want to see you work that booty of yours just like this." She counted the beat and showed them the one, two, three-thrust, one, two, three-thrust, and added four squats.

After repeating the routine twice, she unpaused the music and made eye contact with the women through the mirror. "Ready to—"

A new addition to her class stood out like…like a hot guy in a Zumba class. Normally she was aware when someone came in late, but she had been concentrating on her new routine and didn't see the man with the short, sandy brown hair and delicious five o'clock shadow in the back of the room arrive.

"Welcome." She plastered on a bright smile. "If you can't keep up with the class, it's okay. As long as your body is in motion and you're having fun, you're doing it right." She clapped her hands and danced her way through Katy Perry, doing her best to keep her mind on the next steps and not the handsome man's eyes on her spandex-clad butt.

***

Sweet on You

Trent

The rat bastard was going to die. And Trent was going to enjoy killing him. Losing a bet was one thing, having to endure two weeks of Zumba—whatever the hell that was—with a room full of soccer moms was another.

His gym in the Old Port offered girly classes like this, but there was no way in hell he could show his face there. He figured going to a place on the other side of town and signing up for an early morning class would be his best way to avoid his usual crowd. The guys he knew wouldn't be caught dead here, and the girls he dated would never wake up this early in the morning.

Not that he knew first-hand. Trent didn't do sleepovers, partly because he was used to waking up at the crack of dawn to start the baking, and mostly because he didn't do relationships. And the best way to avoid commitments was to be one hundred percent up front with the women he dated.

After avoiding conversation and eye contact with the young girl at the reception desk, making no apology for being late to the class, he trudged toward the music. Trent could feel his manhood shrinking at the sound of a woman hollering directions over the chick music. He felt sorry for his sister, who would soon be a widow but, best friend or not, there was no way in hell Brian would ever live to see the light of another day.

The room screamed high-maintenance diva with its pink glow and girly script on the wall. And was that vanilla he smelled? It was one of Trent's favorite scents, but not for a gym. Where was the sweat, the grunting, the AC/DC, the clank of weights and dumbbells?

Slipping in at the back of the room, he gawked at the crowd of women. They ranged from young to old, thin to slightly overweight. The younger women turned toward him and made no attempt to hide their surprise at his presence. An obvious party crasher, Trent was insecure for the first time in…ever.

The woman upfront hollering out directions was obviously the instructor. Lost in her element, she moved like no one was watching, the world her stage. The music suddenly stopped and the women flowed like synchronized swimmers to their water bottles, which rested on the strategically placed shelves on the walls.

He watched the instructor with the hot body do an erotic dance solely for him. Okay, maybe it wasn't supposed to be erotic and maybe it wasn't just for him, but it sure as hell felt that way. She wasn't the anorexic bimbo he imagined the instructor looking like. This woman was tall and fit, her thighs were strong, her arms sculpted, and her butt...*H-o-l-y crap*. He could definitely bounce a quarter off her beautiful, curvaceous backside. It was as smooth as the fondant he fitted over the mayor's birthday cake. It wasn't his fault she called attention to it. Didn't she just ask the class to watch her "booty"?

The instructor's hair swayed with her moves. He could imagine wrapping his hand around it and pulling her head back as he explored her neck. Trent couldn't make out her facial features too well from the back of the room, but he knew she wasn't ugly. No, a woman with a sweet, yet authoritative voice and a body that could grace the cover of the swimsuit edition of *Sports Illustrated* had to have at least passable looks.

And then she turned. *Passable my ass.* The woman was flawless. A huge smile enhanced her cheekbones and somehow made her eyes larger instead of smaller as she welcomed him to class. Trent had suddenly died and gone to Zumba heaven. *Damn.* He needed to redirect his one-track mind before he tented his shorts. The next forty-five minutes dragged on as he awkwardly tried to mimic her moves, imagining them alone, bodies melded, doing a private dance of their own.

***

Rayne

As expected, the moms sped off to return home to their children and spouses and the single women flocked to the newcomer. Rayne pretended to ignore the excitement as she drank her water and dried her face on her towel. It would be rude of her not to introduce herself to her newest and unexpected student, although he was probably gay. Straight men never came into her studio unless they were picking up their wife or girlfriend.

Wiping her hand on her towel, she smiled and walked over to the poor man. The women obviously hadn't figured out he played for the other team and were making spectacles of themselves, touching his arms and sticking their chests out like peacocks showing off their feathers.

"Sorry to put an end to the social hour, ladies, but the next class is due in ten minutes and I need to Swiffer the floors. You sticking around to help clean up?" She smiled as Zoe, the leader of the group of college girls already bored during their summer vacation, fled first. The other women slouched as if defeated and walked off as well. "So." Rayne turned to the hunky man with incredible calves and stretched out her hand. "I'm Rayne Wilde. What did you think of the class?"

"Good." The man's gaze darted everywhere except at her, obviously expecting her to hit on him too. Finally noticing her hand, he stuck his out and made contact, sending rivers of electric lust through her body.

"First time?" She released his hand and fought off the temptation to squeeze his biceps.

"What?"

She laughed at his nervousness. "First time taking a Zumba class?"

"Oh, yeah." He lifted the bottom of his shirt and used it to wipe off his face, revealing an amazing set of washboard abs. She blamed the moisture between her legs on the intense morning workout.

Between his hair, damp with perspiration, the scruff on his face, and the amazingly vivid deep-set green eyes, the man was simply breathtaking. *Too bad.* Damn ovary crusher.

"Trent...my name's Trent."

"Well, nice to meet you, Trent. I hope you come

back to another class. Or if you didn't find Zumba to your liking, we offer many other classes: yoga, Pilates, kickboxing, swing dancing—only you'd need to bring your partner for that one." She smiled at her creative way of sneaking the partner bit in.

"Yeah, okay. Um, I think I'll stick with Zumba for now and see what happens." He turned and headed for the door. "It was, uh, nice meeting you, Rayne."

She watched him leave and couldn't help noticing his spectacular, tight booty. What a shame it didn't swing her way.

***

Trent

"You're in early."

"And I'll say the same to you, Marie." Trent looked up briefly from the tray of wild berry muffins he was filling and eyed his best employee.

"I thought you weren't coming in until after seven, so I came in to do the muffins. Had I known you'd be here at four even though you—" Marie stopped short when he lifted his head and scowled at her. "Oh, dear. I'm not supposed to know about that, am I?"

"You won't miss your son when I kill him, will you? He's easily replaceable. You can be my mom instead."

Marie laughed. "You've always been a son to me, dear. Toss your batch of muffins in the oven and then go. You don't want to be late for your morning workout." The twinkle in her eye didn't go unnoticed as she carried her stout, five-foot-nothing frame toward the swinging doors to the front of the bakery.

"I still have time to whip up a batch of whoopee pies. I'll need you to fill them, though," he said to her retreating back.

Trent hadn't told Brian about the hot instructor, so there was no way Marie knew about her, but he didn't expect his *former* best friend to squeal about their stupid bet to his mommy. It was embarrassing enough having his sister Claire know and tease him mercilessly. But Marie? She was his employee, dammit. Although she often didn't act it. He'd never admit it, but he actually enjoyed it when Marie tossed an order or two at him. God knows he never had anyone around to dish it out at him growing up.

Sighing, he measured out flour, sugar, and cocoa powder and the rest of the ingredients he knew by heart, and incorporated them in the mixer. He cleaned up his mess while the cakes baked and after an hour, untied his white apron and tossed it in the laundry bin. Already dressed in running shorts and a t-shirt, Trent thought the three-mile run to the fitness center would help take his mind off Rayne.

Although in truth, the run actually gave him *more* time to think about the way her tight black shorts molded to her butt and thighs. His hands itched to be trapped between her bright pink spandex sports bra and what promised to be soft breasts.

Trent pushed his legs harder and faster, willing

Junior to stay low and in control.

***

By the third class, Trent had a few of the routines almost down. Granted, he sucked. Sucked big time, but being forced to stare at the sexiest gift God ever created for one hour three days a week wasn't so bad. He had three more classes next week before he'd be done with this stupid bet. And then he would ask Rayne out.

He couldn't date her while taking her class. It felt…weird. After brushing off the unwanted advances of Zoe and her clan, he hung around and helped Rayne pick up stray water bottles while she Swiffered the floor.

"Thanks for your help. Keep this up and I'll throw in an extra week for you."

"No," Trent said a little too quickly. "Six classes are enough."

"Six? Why only six? I'm not saying you're not in excellent shape, but you should try sticking with it for a while. It gets easier to follow each time. Promise."

Ouch. Okay, so she noticed he sucked. Not a great first impression to make. "No, it's just that I, uh…" Since when did his mouth struggle to form a cohesive sentence or, hell, a smooth line for a beautiful woman? "I have a pretty busy work schedule coming up and this was something I wanted to try. I committed to six classes and I'm not a quitter. Zumba isn't my…thing." He tossed the bottles in a recycling box by the door.

"Oh yeah?" she said, smiling. "What exactly is your *thing?*"

Was she flirting with him? If so, it would be the first time all week. "Well, for workouts I usually run, rock climb, kayak in the summer, ski in the winter. That sort of thing."

"Cool. I've never been rock climbing. It's definitely on my bucket list."

"I'll take you. There are plenty of great spots around here." *Whoa, did I just ask her out?*

"Sure! Great, that would be fun!" Rayne's ponytail swung as she zipped through the room, dry-mopping the floor.

If she could be casual, so could he. "Yeah, let me know when you're free and I'll arrange it."

"Cool."

Cool as in I can't wait to rip your clothes off *cool?* He wanted to ask her. Trent followed Rayne out the door and toward the front desk, where he was shocked and embarrassed to see Brian.

"Hey, man. Thought I'd check out the fitness center. See the class you've been raving about." Brian smirked while rocking the baby stroller.

Trent hadn't mentioned the class and he definitely hadn't mentioned which fitness center he went to, or anything about the hot instructor who was currently the subject of Brian's scrutiny. The beaming smile and knowing expression on his face pissed him off.

"Pardon my man's manners. I'm Brian." He reached out his hand to Rayne, who immediately accepted it and didn't seem fazed when Brian held on longer than appropriate. Her eyes were focused elsewhere. The baby overshadowed them both.

"I'm Rayne," she said with little interest in the men, then squatted down by the stroller. "And who is this beautiful girl?" She stroked the baby's cheek with her knuckles and seemed to forget about everyone else in the room. Brian was right. Babies were a total chick magnet.

"This," Trent said as he reached down to unbuckle his goddaughter, "is Faith." He scooped up the tiny baby, held her to his chest and kissed her sweet-smelling, downy hair. Maybe he was scum, using Faith as a ploy to weaken Rayne, but it seemed to work.

"Oh, she's beautiful," Rayne cooed.

"Would you like to hold her?"

"Can I?" she questioned, her gaze darting from Trent to Brian.

"Sure." The hand-off was exactly as he hoped. Rayne's fingers caressed his arms as she reached under the little bundle and scooped the baby to her chest. Okay, so maybe she didn't *caress* his arms, but the touch felt close, nonetheless. And electrifying.

Brian and Trent stood mesmerized by the sight. Perfection.

"Excuse me, Rayne?" the receptionist called from behind the front desk.

"What's up, Sarah?" Rayne looked at the receptionist and continued to stroke the baby's head, rubbing her cheek against Faith's soft hair.

"Your seven-thirty private lesson cancelled. Seems Ms. McIntyre is down with the flu."

"Oh, that's too bad. I guess I'll do some

paperwork until my nine o'clock class starts." She returned her full attention to Faith.

Brian cleared his throat. "Yeah, uh, Kip, did you get my message? I got called in to work. Think you can watch the baby for a couple hours?" Brian smirked, looking from Rayne—who was oblivious to the world around her except for the baby in her arms—to Trent. And just like that Brian made it back to Best Friend status.

"Sure. Take your time. Faith and I will go for a walk around the Back Cove." He waited for Rayne to say something, but she was too caught up with the baby magic. He'd have to try harder. Trent caught Brian's gaze, then nodded to the door. When Brian left, Trent turned back to Rayne. "Since, ah, you're off, want to go for a walk with us?"

"What?" Rayne lifted her chocolate eyes to him and his knees nearly buckled. Damn. Zumba was turning him into a freakin' girl.

"I'm on babysitting duty for a few hours. Feel like going for a morning stroll around the cove before your next class? Unless you have a lot of work to do…"

"Oh! I'd love to. Can I push the stroller?"

Laughing, Trent took Faith from Rayne's arms and strapped the baby back in her carriage. "Sure."

"Great. Let me clear a few things here first."

He waited in the lobby area while she talked quietly with Sarah at the front desk and then she jogged over to him wearing the biggest, sexiest smile he'd seen in ages.

"Move over, papa. This mama bear wants a turn." She elbowed him away from the stroller and pushed it as if she did this every day.

"I never thought to ask…do you have any kids?" Damn if he'd tangle himself with a single mother looking for a stand-in father. Trent held the door open as she followed the stroller outside into the warm June morning air.

"Me? No. I do want a big family someday. Lots and lots of kids. I love them."

Too bad. "I can tell." He'd rather know up front what the woman's expectations were. It made things less complicated later on. Knowing she'd be the type, Trent tucked his thumbs in the waistband of his shorts and sighed in disappointment.

"You're pretty good with babies." Her cute dimple and infectious giggle perked him up—the upper and lower extremities.

"And you know this how?" He laughed.

"You're a natural. A woman can always tell when a man is nervous around kids. It's obvious how much you love Faith."

"She's the best. I'd never been around babies before, hell, any-aged kid, but Faith makes it easy." And not being responsible for her welfare and happiness helped his aversion to having kids. He could be the loving uncle, but would never have a child of his own. He came from bad blood. Bad genes. And refused to pass them on to someone else.

Rayne stopped walking, put her hand over her chest and glanced up at him. "Wow. I think I'm in love."

Trent pulled back, fear and trepidation cinching his chest. Of course a girl like Rayne would want more than he could offer. Too wrapped up in staring at Faith again, Rayne didn't seem to notice his hesitancy. She continued walking and laughing, waving a hand in the air as she pushed the stroller, asking questions about Faith and telling him about the other classes she taught. Trent would have hit the ground running as soon as she started talking about babies and the white picket fence, but she wasn't pressuring him into being her other half or hinting that she wanted anything to do with him other than smother his goddaughter with attention. Part of him was offended that she wasn't falling all over him. And then she stopped, squatted in front of Faith, and made the same ridiculous raspberry noises with her mouth he'd often see his sister do.

The instant attraction morphed into something else unrecognizable to Trent. Appreciation? Admiration? He hadn't a clue.

They talked and laughed during their hour walk around the cove. He couldn't remember having such a relaxing time with a woman. She wasn't hitting on him and he wasn't hitting on her; they laughed and enjoyed each other's company. It's like they were becoming…friends.

***

Rayne

Her heart danced and twirled during their walk. If Trent Kipson wasn't gay she'd be desperately in love…again…and running to Macy's to pick out a china pattern…again. Maybe he was a gift from heaven. Rayne knew she had issues and fell in and out of love too easily. She wanted to marry and have the house full of babies she so desired. Soon.

Owning and running her fitness studio paid the bills, but her heart wouldn't be complete until she had a child of her own.

Rayne liked being in a relationship, but men seemed to shy away when she started talking about starting a family. She'd fallen for two men who said they wanted the happily ever after with her, yet when it came down to deciding on venues and dates, they got cold feet and strayed. Thankfully falling out of love wasn't hard to do when the men she dated had cheated, didn't want children, wanted no-strings sex, or bored her to death.

However, Trent was different. He was adorably handsome and panty-dropping sexy holding his daughter. It was totally inappropriate, thinking about sex when holding a baby, but wasn't that how they were made? God knew what he was doing when he made Trent. And his boyfriend wasn't too hard on the eyes either.

They talked about sports, movies, Maine, and fitness as they walked. It was a relief not to have to hold her heart at bay or be constantly wondering when he was going to try to shove his hand down her pants. Instead of pondering how long she'd have to date Trent before he popped the question and they had oodles of babies, she focused on getting to know him. Without the added pressure of hoping he'd be her soul mate, Rayne let loose and giggled and snorted like she was hanging with her sisters, not worrying about making a fool of herself.

Rayne knew she didn't have a striking face like her sister Sage, or a cute button nose like her sister Thyme, but she had a great body. Now. She was half the size she was ten years ago.

For the first two months of college, she seriously hated her college roommate. The girl was beautiful, bouncy, and hit it off with all the boys, but she took Rayne under her wing and got her into parties and introduced her to people. By the end of their freshman year, Rayne had lost fifty pounds, learned how to apply the right amount of makeup, and had an in with the "cool kids" on campus.

Once she gained a little self-confidence, life was a breeze. By the end of her sophomore year, she changed her major to health and fitness with a minor in business management. She realized feeling good about her appearance actually helped her come out of her shell and gave her time to enjoy life.

Not that Rayne was a wallflower before her physical transformation; taking care of her sisters and trying to be noticed by her parents had sucked any type of enjoyment out of her. The typical middle child syndrome—needing to please everyone. All she ever wanted was to be loved and to have someone to love.

"How about next week? If the weather is nice we can go rock climbing? I'll take you on some easy cliffs and work our way to the steeper climbs once you're comfortable."

They had circled the trail around the cove and were back at *In Motion,* thus ending their lovely walk. "That sounds awesome. What's your work schedule like? Hey!" She stopped and put her hands on her hips. "You know about me and my work, but you never even told me what you do for a living."

She watched him sigh and stare over her shoulder. Uh oh. Did she offend him? Was he unemployed? A Wal-Mart greeter? A male stripper? The latter, she could imagine.

"I work at a bakery."

"My younger sister is a great baker. Me, not so much. I take it you don't work the morning shift or you wouldn't be at the early Zumba class."

"Actually, I put in a few hours before coming here. I should probably head back to work soon."

"Wow, you're a workaholic then? Boss must love you."

Trent laughed. "Some days. I actually own the bakery. Sweet Spot."

"Cute name."

"You've never heard of it?"

Rayne shrugged. "No. I don't eat out much unless I'm doing a girls' thing with my sisters." She smiled. "And I'm a health fanatic. No offense to your bakery, but I don't eat sweets. They're really not a necessary part of one's diet."

He gasped and clutched his chest. "Ouch. An arrow through my heart. I don't think I could make it through a day without something sweet to tide me over." He winked flirtatiously at her and she laughed.

"If you say so. I'll stick to coffee and an apple. A green smoothie is as sweet as I get."

"Oh, honey," he drawled and snaked an arm around her shoulders. "I'm going to convert you.

Just watch."

He pecked her cheek and took over stroller duty, walking away from her and around the building to the parking lot.

"Oh, no honey. I'm going to convert *you,*" she mumbled, fanning herself with her hand.

Chapter Two

Rayne

"He's gonna break your heart, Ray-Ray," Rayne's older and man-hating sister Sage said while rolling up her piece of sushi.

"It's not like I'll actually convert him. It's only my wishful thinking. He's obviously in love with his boyfriend. I still really like him. As a friend," Rayne emphasized when Sage gave her the death stare.

"I know you, hun. You're going to obsess over this guy—"

"Trent."

"Trent. And then fall in love knowing he doesn't swing your way. Then you'll come crying to me, and I'll soothe and console and we'll have a bucket of margaritas while I try not to say 'I told you so,' and then you'll be in love with the next hottie to cross your path two weeks later."

Rayne would have been furious with her sister, had she not been right.

"It's not your fault you wear your heart on your sleeve." Sage placed the sushi on a rectangle platter and carried it over to the coffee table in her cramped apartment. "It's the only reason I don't kick your ass." She picked up a pair of chopsticks and pointed them at Rayne. "You're a pathetic romantic."

"I prefer the term 'hopeless.'"

"Whatever." Sage sipped her wine and glared at Rayne over the rim of her glass. "You're destined to fall in love, but don't turn so desperate that you do something stupid."

"I won't."

Sage's eyebrow lifted as she snorted.

"Oh please, you've been a love cynic since you were five and Tommy Whitehouse refused to share his chocolate ice cream cone with you," Rayne teased, and then sunk her mouth into one of Sage's famous sushi rolls.

"Love isn't on my agenda. And you know how I stick with my agendas."

"You've told me the pitiful story of little Tommy a dozen times during girls' nights out, and I don't buy your agenda crap for a second. You're scared to fall in love, and you turn all OCD to play interference."

Sage's life was planned to the minute. She had lists, agendas, Blackberries, iPads, laptops, iPhones and back-up systems to her back-up systems to organize her every move. And true, nowhere on her lists did she write "Fall in love." Rayne knew when Sage was ready she'd write it on a list and *snap,* it would happen. She knew how to play up her strengths, which was what made her a fabulous event planner.

"Whatever," Sage said. "Back to you. What's the deal with Kevin, anyway?"

"I told you already," Rayne said around a mouthful of fish.

"Yeah. A month ago you said you knew he didn't really love you, and you broke it off. No big tears over him. So what gives? Why are you going out with him tomorrow night?"

Rayne cringed and hid her face in her glass of wine.

"Didn't think I'd find out about the date, huh?"

"Well, he showed up at work and sort of asked me out to dinner. I felt bad turning him down in front of Sarah and the other girls."

Sage snorted. "If Mr. Hot and Hunky Zumba Boy wasn't gay, would you have said yes to your bodybuilder?"

Rayne shrugged.

"Bullshit. You're a one-man woman. You're only going out with Kevin again because you know you can't have Mr. Zumba."

"Maybe," Rayne said into her glass.

"Definitely."

"Yeah."

***

Trent

Not wanting to appear too anxious, Trent walked through the doors of *In Motion* three minutes after eight.

"Hey, right on time!" Rayne said with a bounce and a smile.

He'd been sitting in the parking lot for ten minutes having a heart-to-heart with Junior, telling him to tone it down a bit, but couldn't blame his head—either of them—for swelling. Rayne made him smile and laugh and, hell, his body vibrated with need when she was around. He hoped she wouldn't notice the strain against his zipper. Somehow Trent managed to make it through all six Zumba classes without completely embarrassing himself. Well, his moves may have been somewhat humiliating, but concentrating on where and how to shuffle his feet, arms and *booty* kept—sort of—his mind off the sweet booty in the front of the room and helped keep him from making a complete spectacle of himself.

"A slight change of plans." Her smile dropped, giving him great pleasure in knowing how excited she was to see him. "Nothing major. It looks like a storm is rolling in. It's too dangerous to be out on the rocks, so I thought we'd go over to the rock climbing gym up in Auburn. It's usually where people go to familiarize themselves with the ropes, footing, and all before climbing outside."

"Oh! That sounds like fun." She beamed, and she hopped up and down, causing a stir in his cargo shorts.

"Ready?"

"As I'll ever be. Bye, Sarah. See you tomorrow," she called to her receptionist.

Conversation flowed easily during the thirty-minute drive. If Rayne was nervous at being with him or about climbing, she sure didn't show it. It was a surprisingly refreshing change to be with a woman who wasn't constantly putting the moves on him or making dull conversation.

When they got to the gym, he greeted the employees and told Ted, the manager, he'd handle Rayne's orientation. Since he volunteered from time to time with their Overnight Survival Training program and instructed one of the afterschool junior climbing teams, they usually gave him free rein.

"Wow. This place is so cool. I can't believe I've never done this before."

He watched Rayne as she twirled around and took in her surroundings. More than 5,000 square feet of rock-like textured climbing surfaces and thousands of grips and stances braced the walls. Belayers were scattered throughout the center, calling to their climbers.

"Okay. Let's get you suited up." He nudged her left foot so she could step into the harness.

"Um, are you coming with me?" Rayne fiddled with the strapping around her waist.

He saw hesitation in her eyes. His manhood grew ten degrees—figuratively, not literally…yet. He stood and gently elbowed the flat stomach he'd been admiring for a week, and taunted, "You're not afraid, are you?"

"No. Not really. But I thought you were going to be next to me." And his ego—and his manhood—rose another ten degrees. At this rate he'd never fit into his harness.

"I'm going to be your belayer." She scrunched up her cute nose in confusion. "I'm going to hold the rope and call out directions. All you have to think about is where to put your hands and feet. Look for the holds, the stances."

"Eh?"

He chuckled and walked her closer to the wall. "This is called a hold. You *hold* on to it. This is a stance. You put your feet on it and climb. Simple as that."

"How about you climb first and I'll…belay you?"

Oh, the innuendos. "Not a chance, sweetheart. I'm your safety net."

"Gee, that's reassuring. What happens if you don't catch me?"

"First, I don't need to catch you because you aren't going to fall. Second, these ropes…" he stopped to pull them through a carabineer, "and this clip will keep you safe. Even if you slip or let go of the wall, you won't fall down. You'll just dangle in the air."

"Then how do I get down?" She nibbled her bottom lip, and he pictured his lips and teeth finishing the job for her.

"I'll slowly let the rope out. You'll go into a squat position and bounce your feet off the wall until you hit the bottom. Softly," he reassured her. "Trust me. Nothing will happen to you. This is very safe."

Letting out a breath she probably didn't realize she was holding, Rayne pulled up the harness. "Okay, Mr. Hot Shot. Let's do it."

It wasn't like he tried to grope her ass, but he did have to make sure the harness fit tightly around her legs, butt, and waist. If his touching bothered her, she didn't show it. Trent made a growl when Junior twitched. His knuckles brushed across her backside and traced a path up to her waist and around to her stomach. It was subtle, but he thought he sensed her going tense as he reached through her legs to pull the strap around. Knowing he was treading on dangerous territory, Trent quickly finished tightening her harness and stepped back. "You'll have fun. Promise."

With her cheeks flushed, she nodded and surveyed the wall. It wasn't the easiest wall but wasn't Mt. Katahdin either. With her upper body strength, Trent knew she could physically handle it.

Locking his feet in his stance, he pulled in the excess rope as Rayne began to climb. The woman had focus, that was for sure. She never looked down and didn't ask for any help and climbed to the top like Catwoman. *Damn, erase that picture out of your mind right now, Kipson!* He did not need to picture her in a sexy, skimpy, tight catsuit. It was bad enough that the two globes of her butt were accentuated thanks to the climbing harness. Again, not his fault he *had* to keep his eyes glued to her butt. That was the job of the belayer. Oh…so many puns formed in his mind, but he wouldn't go there, either.

Before he knew it, she was at the top ringing the bell and hollering, "I did it! Trent, I did it!"

"I knew you could, sweetheart. Now grab the rope with both hands as I let you down nice and easy. Place both feet on the wall like I showed you."

Rayne grabbed the rope and he watched her

bounce to the floor. Before he could drop the ropes she threw herself in his arms.

"That was the coolest, bestest trip I've ever had. Oh my God, I want to do it again!" She hugged him again, then pulled back to hop up and down, her chest moving deliciously, making it impossible not to stare.

"Absolutely. Want to try a steeper climb?"

"Yes!" She let go of his hold and stepped back. "Wait. It's your turn now. Show me how to belay." Rayne started unbuckling her harness.

"Easy now." He put his hand over hers, enjoying the heat of their bodies and feeling the racing of her pulse. "Keep that on. You can climb as many walls as you'd like. I've done this a thousand times."

"I'm going to watch you this time and then I'll go again. Can you climb that one?" She pointed to the Everest wall.

"If that's what you want." Leave it to her to challenge him with the most difficult, steepest climb. He'd mastered it years ago, so he wasn't worried, but he didn't want to come off cocky.

"It looks hard. Have you done it before?"

Mind. Gutter. Get out. "A few times."

"Did you fall?"

"I have slipped, yes. Only you don't fall if you have a strong belayer." He winked, then called to one of the employees, "Cote. I'm going up. Can you spot me?"

"Hmph. I'm offended. I could totally spot you." She crossed her arms over her perky breasts and almost pouted. The excitement in her face didn't allow her to frown that much.

"I hope you do." He winked and double-checked his gear. Cote did a quick spot-check as well before Trent started his climb.

Careful not to show off too much and accidentally slip, Trent climbed like Spider-Man, clinging to the overhang.

"Oh my God, Trent! You're practically upside down. Don't fall."

He smiled and tried not to laugh, which would probably cause him to lose his grip and his cool status. The woman was worried about him, and damn if that didn't boost his ego just a touch. Rayne deserved a show, and a show she was going to get. Letting his feet fall, he dangled, gripping tightly on to the holds. Using his forearms to pull himself up, he slowly lifted his body to the next tier, bringing his right leg nearly over his head. Yeah, he was that good, and yeah, he wanted her to know it. He prayed his legs didn't break out in an Elvis and start shaking in front of his fan club.

Rayne gasped from below, and Trent did all he could to clear his mind of her and get himself out of this precariously challenging situation. Reaching over his head for another pull, his shaking arms carried his body over the last lip and up to the ceiling.

He may have pushed it a bit on the last stretch. His new sudden fame had kept him busy in the bakery and off the rocks for the past few weeks.

The whooping and cheering below caused a sudden spectacle around the gym. Everest had been empty all morning; it took months of training to climb this wall, and most enthusiasts climbed outside in the summer. As the onlookers slowly made their way over to Rayne and Trent's private corner, he called out to Cote and slid down the rope until he hit the ground.

"Holy crap, Trent. Or should I call you Peter Parker?" Her Godiva eyes glowed and her sweet, shiny lips parted into a bright smile, enhancing her perfectly white teeth.

Damn, he'd like to take her mouth for a test drive. "Your turn."

"Oh no. I can't do this wall." She backed away from him.

Trent reached out and grabbed her arm. "Not Everest, but I think you can climb Katahdin." He led her toward an intermediate wall and prayed the group of women at the Shawnee Peak wall wouldn't come over. Unfortunately, they recognized him, puffed out their feathers and sauntered over, not caring that he was with another woman.

"Hey, you're that hot baker guy, aren't you?"

"Um, I…uh…" He glanced at Rayne, who raised her eyebrow in question. Trent couldn't tell if she was miffed or amused.

"You are," the tall redhead fawned. "Can I have your autograph?" She sized him up with predatory eyes. "I guess you can't do that now. If I swing by the bakery later, will you make me something special?"

The woman had no shame. "Stop by anytime. We always have specials." He turned to recheck Rayne and the redhead didn't stop talking. And flirting. He didn't know if he was more embarrassed for himself or her. She finally got the hint and left after he let out a few grunts and one-word responses.

"Sorry about that," he mumbled while pulling on Rayne's rope.

"I didn't realize bakers were famous. Is there something I don't know about you? Are you a rock star on the side? Retired child actor?"

Trent laughed. "No, nothing that exciting. Sweet Spot made it into a few magazines and news spots. It sort of put us on the map. I mean, we were doing well before all this hoopla, but I can't complain about the business the media has raked in for me."

And the possible job of a lifetime. Felicia Cortez called him last night and emailed him his itinerary. By the end of July, he'd be flying into LAX and touring the Cooking Network's studio in Burbank. If things went well, he'd be the new host of *So You Think You Can Bake,* a spin-off of *Cupcake Wars.* If he got the job, Trent would travel across the country sampling and judging different bakers' concoctions and might even get an opportunity to film a few episodes of his own. Trent hadn't told his sister or Brian about the offer yet; he'd wait until he had the contract in hand.

"Very cool. That's every business owner's dream, yet you don't seem too thrilled about it."

"It's good. Most of it. That part," he shrugged toward the redhead, "is the annoying bit."

***

Rayne

Handsome and modest. Yeah. Rayne was totally over-the-top, head-over-heels crushing over Trent Kipson. It wasn't love. It could be, if only...She watched his strong, yet somehow delicate hands make fast work of the contraption around his waist. It looked like a glorified diaper and she felt ridiculous in it, but it did amazing things for her new crush.

The harness cupped his butt and enhanced his front side, revealing a very nice package. One she'd never get to open, but a girl could dream. In elementary school, she dreamt about Harry Potter turning her into a princess. Then it was Channing Tatum doing a magical dance just for her. Her most recent infatuation—as Sage called them—was Chris Pratt. He and Trent shared the same boyish smile.

Oh yeah, she was totally doomed. And smitten. And he was totally off limits. Which was probably a good thing.

"You all right?" The movie star lookalike asked, slowly standing from his crouch. If Trent wasn't...Trent, and they weren't in a public place, the seductive stance and alluring eyes would have her stripping off her shirt and jumping into his arms.

She had to remind herself that he liked men— who could blame him—and they were in a very public place. *Damn.* He caught her staring and that was mortifying.

"No, I'm good. I'm getting my game face on before I take a nose-dive off this cliff."

Trent chuckled. "No nose-diving on my watch.

And it's just a wall. No cliffs in sight."

She snorted and rolled her eyes. "Yeah, maybe to you, but you probably do 100 pull-ups a day."

Without confirming or denying his workout ritual, which sadly no longer involved Zumba, he smirked and put his strong hands on her shoulders. "I got your back sweetheart. Nothing to fear."

Sighing, she reached out for her safety rope and walked toward the looming wall. Without turning around she called, "Just so you know, payback's a bitch."

The deep laugh from below made her heart quiver and nearly made her hands shake. No, he expected her to climb the wall, and if she had any hopes of *converting* him, she had to stay strong.

***

Trent

"Mmm, I haven't had a lobster roll in months. This is the best surprise lunch ever." Rayne closed her eyes and groaned, making an entirely too erotic scene at their picnic table by the ocean. The storm had passed through quickly as they typically did in the summer, leaving behind the smell of fresh rain and salty air.

Trent held himself back from plunging his tongue into her mouth. He'd never envied a piece of food before but damn, he wished he was on the roll and her mouth was…*wow, don't go there.* Adjusting his crotch—which was thankfully hidden under the table—he finished off his beer and signaled the waitress.

"Done with lunch? Would you like dessert? We have amazing strawberry shortcake or maybe you'd like a scoop of ice cream with gooey...hot...chocolate sauce..." The young girl who worked at the Lobster Shack was ignoring Rayne and pouring out an obvious invitation to Trent. It made him sick. Couldn't she see he was with a woman? Even though Rayne made it clear she wasn't interested in anything romantic, she had to be offended by the sexual innuendos. Was it something in the water that had all the women pawing after him like mares in heat? Spending time with Rayne over the past few weeks had been somewhat refreshing. While he wanted to get in her pants, not having to worry about saying the right thing or sending the right or wrong messages of commitment felt pretty damn good too.

It was the first time in...ever that he could be himself around a woman. Brian would have his ass if he ever heard Trent admit to being anything but relaxed around sexy curves. He didn't trust women. Not after the way his mother up and left him and Claire. And his history with women was only proof that all—well, most—were after one thing. Very few had a genuine soul. Very few were like his sister.

Or Rayne. Damn. He wouldn't put her in the same category as Claire. His feelings toward her were so not sisterly, but he also didn't want to ruin the best friendship he'd had since meeting Brian in Little League. And he sure as hell never had a *friendship* with a woman.

Without taking his eyes off of Rayne, he said, "Check, please." The waitress stormed off in a huff.

Rayne had yet to stop by the bakery, claiming she didn't eat sugar and that it went straight to her thighs. *Yeah, I'd like to go straight to your thighs.* Shaking his lusty thoughts out of his head, he smiled at her.

As if reading his thoughts about friendship, she said, "So tell me more about Brian. How long have you known him?"

"Since we were kids. We played ball together and I spent more time at his house growing up than in my own. I think of his mom, Marie, as my own. She even works at the bakery with me. Pretty much runs the place. I don't know what I would do without her. Or Brian. But if you ever tell him I said that I'll completely deny it."

Rayne laughed and reached across the table, placing her hand on top of his. "Today was a great day. Thank you for bringing me rock climbing."

He clasped her hand and brought her knuckles to his lips. "I'm really proud of you. You'd never know today was your first climb." Trent pulled her gently to her feet and led her to his SUV. After unlocking the passenger side door, he opened it, but Rayne stood in between the door and the car as if waiting for…a kiss? No, he couldn't go there.

Last week during a jog around the bay, she'd told him she was a hopeless romantic. That she always fell in love at first sight and how freeing it was to spend time with him knowing nothing would come of it. At first he didn't think he'd heard her correctly, because she kept on jogging as if they were discussing the weather. Rayne didn't elaborate as to why she felt so sure nothing sexual or romantic would come of their relationship, and he didn't know whether to be offended or grateful.

Instead of correcting her, he had let her ramble about her past relationships. Two failed engagements, four cheaters, and one forty-year-old virgin. How any sane man could cheat on her was beyond him. Apparently she fell in love too fast. Rayne didn't lay blame for the failed relationships in her life and took responsibility for her own actions.

"I fall hard and then I get clingy. I can't help it. Being in love is such an amazing feeling and it makes me happy." She had turned toward him and smiled as they jogged, her ponytail flailing back and forth, her legs never missing a stride. "It's completely euphoric. Better than sex. Sex lasts…ten, fifteen minutes, but being in love lasts forever. Well, maybe not forever in my life. Yet. It will someday, though. I'm confident there's the perfect guy out there waiting for me. Which is another reason I'm so grateful for our friendship." She smiled at him again and for a brief second he thought he saw something more than platonic interest. And then it deflated as quickly as an undercooked soufflé. "It shows me that not all guys are asses."

While his pace had slowed, hers had stayed constant. It was then he knew he couldn't make a pass at her. What the hell was wrong with him anyway? Why wasn't she attracted to him? Rayne wanted and deserved the happily ever after. The

Sweet on You

Cape Cod house with the white picket fence, two kids. A dog. Stability.

Trent was anything but stable. And he liked his life that way. He supposed that was why Rayne didn't throw herself at him like all the others. Living in the Old Port meant he could stumble out of bed and into work at the crack of dawn or walk down the street at night to a pub for a nice cold one, play a game of darts or pool. Hang out with the guys or meet a woman.

And pretty soon he'd be working the dream job. Traveling, meeting new people, baking and meeting other bakers across the country.

Other than Sweet Spot, he had no commitments. The lease on his brownstone had to be renewed every six months, the lease on his SUV every two years. Just like Maine's motto, it was *the way life should be.*

Willing his libido to cool, he bent down and pecked her cheek. "Today was fun, but I'm wondering what you have up your sleeve for us for next week. Should I be worried about your *payback's a bitch* statement, or did I do all right?"

"Oh, I owe you big for today. Next week's adventure's gonna knock your socks off."

He'd prefer it if she knocked his shorts off, but he'd take what he could get. "Don't forget about the Fourth of July at my place. We'll grill around five but come whenever. The fireworks show from my deck is amazing. And you won't have to worry about the gridlock of traffic when it's all over."

"I'm looking forward to it. What can I bring?"

"Nothing. Just yourself."

"Can I...uh...bring a friend? I sort of forgot that I had already made tentative plans. I can—"

"Absolutely. Bring a friend. The more the merrier."

She smiled shyly and slid into the front seat.

Trent couldn't wait to meet Rayne's friend. Hopefully she could fill him in on some unanswered questions.

Chapter Three

Rayne

"I'm going out of my mind, Sage." Rayne hung her head upside down and wrapped her wet hair in her towel. Standing up, she put her hands on her hips and shook her heavy head. "I'm going freaking nuts. I can't believe I let Kevin talk me into this again."

"You said it. You are freaking nuts. The guy's a loser. There's a very good reason you broke up with him—"

"He dumped me."

"Because you were about to bust his ass for cheating on you." Sage stretched out her right foot on Rayne's bed and admired her freshly painted toes.

"We never said we were exclusive."

"Raynie, he told you he loved you. And you *said* you loved him…"

Sage didn't need to state her opinion. Again. Rayne knew exactly how Sage felt about her love life. It didn't help that her sister didn't believe in love. The trail of men she left in her dust could spread from coast to coast. That they had completely differing views on relationships and matters of the heart and were still close was surely a testament to their sisterly bond. She only wished Sage would get along better with Thyme. Thyme had always been the flighty sister, and Sage's OCD had no tolerance for it.

"You're a fool but I love you. And you know I don't throw that word around," Sage grumbled. "If you feel obligated to keep this stupid date with Kevin, at least you're bringing him to Trent's. I haven't met this guy yet but it sounds like he cares a lot about you. I'd like to get his take on the stupid oaf. I may stop by Sweet Spot after and—"

"Don't you dare, Sage Lavender Wilde. You stay out of this!"

Sage brought her dainty foot closer and painted a second coat of fuchsia nail polish on her toenails. "I'm just saying…"

"No, you're not. You love to meddle. It's probably why you're the best event planner in southern Maine." Rayne loosened her towel, slipped on a pair of shorts and pulled a tank top over her head. "Plan, plan, plan. That's what you do. But you can't plan my life, Sage."

"Oh, don't I know it," Sage snorted. "Trust me, I've tried."

"And you can't meddle."

"Oh, that I can do. As your best friend and favorite sister, I've earned that privilege. I'm looking out for your best interests."

"Whatever." Rayne walked back into the bathroom and turned on her hair dryer. Going out with Kevin was definitely a mistake, even though she made it clear to him they were just friends now. As a professional bodybuilder, Kevin was more interested in the size of his muscles and his spray tan than he was Rayne. Kevin liked her profession and how she looked on his arm. His love for fitness was what got them together in the first place, but his obsession with it, and himself, and other women, is what drove her away. She knew she was using him as a distraction but he wouldn't care. They'd go out on the Fourth, hang out with Trent and Brian, watch the fireworks, and she'd go home alone.

Pulling her hair up in a clip, Rayne stuck her head out the bathroom door and called to Sage. "If I somehow cave and let Kevin come home with me tomorrow night, you have my permission to smack me over the head, lock me in my apartment, and never let me date again. Promise."

"Oh, you're on, girlfriend. After tomorrow night, you'll never see that bastard again. Why you are keeping this date is beyond me…No, it's actually not. You're good to a fault." Sage got up and put the nail polish on Rayne's dresser. "You're too sweet, always trying to make everyone happy. But don't even think about making Kevin happy, got it?"

"Yes, ma'am."

After Sage left, Rayne made a quick grocery list and headed to the market to pick up the makings for a fruit salad to bring to Trent's cookout. The last of her groceries loaded, she closed the trunk of her car and was startled to see Brian standing behind her cart.

"I thought that was you. I came over to offer a hand. It looks like you're all set."

"Thanks. Just picking up a few things for tomorrow."

"Yeah, Trent said you're coming to the cookout. Faith will be happy to see you." He laughed.

"Oh, where is the angel?"

"Claire's with her while I help Trent set up for tomorrow. You know he can bake, but did you know he's king of the grill as well? Men have tried to strip him of the title, but I don't mind keeping the barbecue tongs in his hand. All I have to do is sit back and eat."

Rayne chuckled. "I guess that's why you two make the perfect couple."

"What?"

Realizing Brian, too, may not like discussing his sexual status, Rayne backpedaled. "I'm sorry if I overstepped my boundaries. Trent doesn't talk about his sexuality either. I should respect your privacy."

"Okay…" Brian cocked his head and lowered his sunglasses. He was a handsome man as well. She could see why Trent would be attracted to him. "What exactly doesn't he like to discuss?"

"Well…your relationship. I know you were childhood friends, but when did you both realize you were gay?"

Brian started coughing. Clearly he didn't expect her to get so personal.

"Gay?"

Sweet on You

"Forget I said anything. I didn't mean to make you feel uncomfortable. I really admire him…and you. You're both very nice men and such good fathers." Seeing his embarrassment, Rayne pulled her keys from her purse and opened her door. "I'm sorry, Brian. Forget I ever asked. I'll see you tomorrow." She slid into her car and closed the door, hoping she didn't ruin the best relationship she'd ever had.

***

Brian

"And you didn't correct her?" Claire slapped Brian on the arm. "You idiot! The poor girl."

Brian couldn't stop laughing. The tears had finally stopped flowing out of his eyes, but his body still shook with amusement. So, the girl who had Trent all twisted up in knots thought he was gay. This couldn't be any funnier. In truth, Brian had been surprised that Trent could keep his hands off such a hot woman and that she could actually be content with a friendship with Trent. The girls fell at his feet. Hell, he'd won that crazy-ass Zumba bet because Trent couldn't go five minutes without getting hit on.

And the only reason Rayne didn't hit on Trent was because she thought he was gay.

Too. Freakin'. Hilarious. Oh, he'd have fun with this one.

"Brian Smart. Don't you dare. You call my brother right now and tell him about this. He deserves to know. And so does that poor girl. She's going to feel like a fool when she finds out."

"Yeah, yeah, yeah. I'll tell him. Give me some time to enjoy this. She thinks he's gay." Another fit of laughter erupted from his lungs as he wrapped his wife in a bear hug.

"And she thinks you're gay too, Mr. Funnypants."

Shit. That was not funny at all.

***

Trent

It must have been the cloudless, blue sky and flawless eighty-degree day. Or the ocean breeze. Maybe it was the busy morning at the bakery? No, Trent's good mood had nothing to do with weather and finances. And he wouldn't admit that it had anything to do with a gorgeous brunette who'd be entering his home in—he took out his cell phone and checked the time—four minutes.

Trent didn't get nervous. Or excited. No, he was as cool as the frozen watermelon sorbet he made last night. Just chillin'. That was Trent. That was why he stayed in the backyard, pouring lighter fluid over the cold, black briquettes, waiting for the ebony cubes to turn ash gray, and not in the house, pacing and staring out the front window. Not a thing on his mind but grillin' and swillin' and chillin'.

The friend status with Rayne had been going surprisingly well despite the constant cold showers and lack of sex. Granted, he'd prefer friends with benefits, but he'd settle. Nope, no anxiety attack coming on at all.

The doorbell rang and his internal sorbet quickly melted. No longer chillin', now he was sweatin'. Wiping the beads of perspiration off his forehead with his t-shirt—yeah, he was classy too—he quickly turned his back to the sliding door, pretending to be enthralled with his grill and not his newest guest.

And then he heard her voice. So happy. So sweet. She *ohh*ed. Claire must have given her the baby to hold. Trent couldn't make out the words; all he could hear was her smooth-as-milk-chocolate voice cooing to the baby.

Damn. He should have been on baby patrol instead of manning the grill. But no. Nobody touched the meat in his house. Instantly his mind switched to pig status and thought of some meat that he'd let Rayne handle.

Gross. No. He wasn't a pig, but she brought out the teenage boy in him. He'd be lucky if he didn't drool on her over the chicken. Trent lit a match and dropped it in the barbeque pit, enjoying the sudden *whoosh* as the charcoal caught on fire.

The deep baritone of a male voice brought his thoughts back to PG land. Someone else had arrived as well. Figuring it was Cote and Thomas from the Rock Gym, he stayed outside and tended to his meat. Most likely they were ogling Rayne and her friend and had no desire to hang with Trent.

Couldn't blame them, really.

The slider opened and Brian stepped out.

"Dude," he said and slapped Trent on the back.

"We gotta talk. Fast."

Brian furrowed his brows and sucked in his teeth, glancing over his shoulder one more time before turning to face Trent again.

"Rayne? Is she all right?"

Brian blocked his view of the house. Something didn't smell right and it wasn't the charcoal.

***

Brian

Claire was right. Brian would make it up to her tonight after Faith was asleep. *Damn.* He should have told Trent yesterday. Or at least this morning. Brian never would have guessed that Rayne's *friend* would be a *boy*friend. If one could call him a boy. He stood easily at six and half feet and probably weighed in at 250. All muscle. The guy was jacked, not the kind of guy Brian wanted Trent to mess around with.

The Hulk had his hand on Rayne's butt the entire time she was holding Faith. Brian had tried with polite conversation but the dude completely ignored him, instead making his declaration of love to Rayne, going on about the babies they were going to make. She didn't seem to be into the Hulk the way he was into her, but Brian still needed to warn Trent.

Judging by Trent's over-the-top cheerful mood, he was most likely expecting to get lucky tonight. Fireworks could be romantic—Brian knew that first hand. Last Fourth of July was when Claire proclaimed she wanted a baby. And for the next few weeks he was the luckiest guy in the world, his wife wanting it morning, noon, and night. Of course, most of that sexual bliss ended once she got pregnant and threw up for twelve straight weeks.

"Yeah. She's…uh. Fine. I need to tell you something—"

"There you are! Of course I'd find you out at the grill."

Rayne came skipping out the door and into Trent's arms, kissing him on the cheek. A completely platonic kiss for her gay friend.

There was no mistaking the mountain of lust and something a bit deeper in his friend's eyes.

"Hey, there. I'm so glad you came. I can't wait for you to see the fireworks tonight. The view from the yard is—"

"Hey, babe. Do you know where the beer is?"

Brian scrunched his face in concern and peeked at Trent out of one eye. Trent's focused stare bounced from the Hulk to Rayne to Brian, the question in his mind evident.

"Um, I brought water and a bottle of wine—"

"Come on in with me. I'll grab you one," Brian interjected and jogged inside, but not before missing Trent's beady stare. Once in the kitchen, he placated the Hulk with a beer and offered to show him Trent's weight system in the basement. Leaving him down there, he ran upstairs and sought out his wife.

"Help. Distract Rayne while I go talk to Trent." He kissed his wife on the lips, fast and hard. "Don't say it. I know. You were right."

Dashing outside, he plastered on a fake smile and

called to Rayne, "Mind helping Claire with a few things in the kitchen? I know it's totally sexist, but she said she didn't want my help." He laughed, trying to mask his nervousness.

"Absolutely! I'd love to help," the adorable woman said as she went into the house.

***

Trent

As soon as Rayne closed the screen door behind her, Trent grabbed Brian's shirt, pulled him close, and growled, "What the hell is going on?"

"Well, uh…" Brian's gaze was everywhere but at Trent. Guilt flooded his face, and his shoulders sagged.

Trent let him go, keeping a stern watch on him.

"Okay, well, this is actually kind of funny." Brian laughed, not the funny-ha-ha laugh, but a nervous one.

"Spit it out, Bri," Trent growled, picking up his beer bottle.

"Well, I guess there's been some misunderstanding between you and Rayne. She seems to think that you are…that you and I are…" Brian shifted on his feet, made a flailing motion with his hands, and then shoved them in his pockets. "That, well, that you play for the other team."

Trent choked on his beer. "I love women. I've had lots and lots of sex with lots and lots of women. Why the hell would she think that? What did you tell her?"

"I, uh, didn't tell her anything. I ran into her at the grocery store yesterday and she said…some stuff. Before I could correct her she left."

"You couldn't say, 'No, Trent's not gay. He's a freakin' stud'?"

"Um, saying something like that, well, coming from me, would not really help our cause."

"Who's the muscle?"

"Her boyfriend?"

"No." Trent shook his head. "She doesn't have a boyfriend. Or didn't last week."

"They were talking babies and crap inside. Well, he was. Kevin said he—"

"Damn. Stay here." He shoved the tongs and his beer at Brian. "Don't burn my freakin' chicken."

Trent stormed in the house and zeroed in on Rayne. Cote and Thomas were flirting shamelessly with her and Claire in the kitchen. Not caring how cavemanish he looked, he grabbed Rayne by the arm and pulled her down the hall. "Come with me. Now."

Shoving open his bedroom door, he pulled Rayne inside, slamming it behind her, then stalked up to her, pinning her to the wall with his body. Almost. He didn't dare touch her. But he had to fix this mess.

"Trent, what's wrong? You look…" She reached up to touch his face but he grabbed her wrist and pinned it to the wall above her head. Her gasp turned him on far more than it should have. He braced himself, propping his body away from hers.

"I…" he crushed his mouth to hers quickly,

"...am not..." he whispered now, staring down at her pink, wet lips, and slowly brushed them with his mouth. "Gay." He opened his mouth and prayed to God she would let him in. No coaxing necessary. Rayne opened up and gave him free rein.

It was true bliss. Strawberries and cream. He licked her, played with her, and she gave as much as she took. Her free hand fisted his shirt and pulled him closer. Damn. He could do this all day. The bed was five steps behind him. He knew he could dance her over, lay her down, and strip her of her tight denim shorts and sexy-as-sin red tank top. And she'd love every minute of it.

Someone moaned.

Rayne Wilde had lips and a body that were meant for loving—but no, Rayne Wilde was made for more than that. For true love. White knight. House. Kids. Promises. Trent was none of those things and he respected her too much to pretend otherwise. And making out with her like a dog in heat would only fill her head with romantic thoughts. And Trent was anything but romantic. And the exact opposite of relationship material. *Damn.* She molded her body to his, asking—hell, begging—for him to give her more. Rayne didn't deserve this. He couldn't let her think the kiss was anything more than a point being proven. Next thing he knew she'd be picking out flowers for the wedding.

Reluctantly, Trent pulled back and leaned his forehead against hers. "Clear?"

"Wow." Her milk chocolate eyes darkened, and he imagined what they'd look like if he touched more than just her lips.

Yeah, totally shouldn't have done that. She wanted a husband and kids. Badly. And she had a guy in the other room who was probably willing to give her a multitude of babies and the American Dream.

"I'm not, never have been, and never will be. Got it?"

"Hmm?"

"Gay. I'm not gay."

"What?" She seemed to wake up now. Loosening her grip on his shirt, she tried to step back, but the wall prevented her from moving.

Realizing he had her trapped, Trent moved away, allowing her some room.

"You're not gay?"

Trent rubbed both hands up and down his face. "Not even close. Why the hell would you think that?"

If he could only read the thoughts going on in that sexy mind of hers.

"But…Zumba?"

"Zumba? Zumba made you think I was gay?"

"No, well, yeah." She pulled her hands through her hair—which she wore down, and damn if he didn't find that sexy—and sighed. "The only men who have ever taken my class have been…gay."

"We've been friends for over a month, talk almost every day, hang out a few times a week, and you hadn't figured out that I'm not?"

"Well." She was flustered and adorable, her lips begging to be kissed again. "Then there was Faith."

"Faith told you I was gay?"

Rayne laughed. "No." She relaxed a little and finally made eye contact. Damn those silky eyes. They made him think of erotic images of chocolate sauce and sweet whipped cream and all the wonderful ways he and Rayne could experiment and play with. "Brian came in with her and you two seemed so sweet together with the baby. And she looks like him and also like you…I know that doesn't make sense. She couldn't obviously be both of yours but it's clear how much you both love her and each other."

"Faith is my niece, my only relative other than Claire, and I love her dearly. Brian, well, yeah, I love him in the brother way, not…" He gestured with his hand.

"And you dismiss the looks and pick-up lines from so many women like they mean nothing to you. It's like you're embarrassed because they don't know your secret. And the way you treat me…our friendship. You've never treated me like a piece of meat, or like you were trying to get in my pants. I thought you actually wanted to be…friends."

Trent cursed. Friends. The worst F word in the dictionary. She wanted his friendship and so she'd have it. Obviously hurt after years of being raked over the coals by so many men, she didn't need him pawing at her.

"Definitely friends, Rayne. Always friends. I'm sorry I kissed you. I shouldn't have. I just…needed you to know that I'm not...gay. It won't happen again. We're cool, right?"

***

Sweet on You

Rayne

She nodded.

And then the door burst open.

"Kip, sorry I tried to stop her—" Brian called from the hallway.

"Trent, honey! I'm here. I'm so sorry I'm late. I didn't think I'd ever get away from my sister's bridal shower." A beautiful, tall, dark-haired woman waltzed into Trent's bedroom as if she owned the place and kissed him square on the lips. On the same lips that had, not five minutes ago, been making sweet, magical music with her mouth. The same lips that made her lady parts sing and dance and come alive.

"Katrina," Trent said.

"Trent, sorry, man. I tried to warn her—"

"Oh, please, Brandon."

"Brian."

"Brian, whatever. I know my way around here."

Seeming quite uncomfortable, Trent introduced them. "Katrina, this is Rayne. Rayne, Katrina."

"Uh, nice to meet you?" Rayne said, not sure of this woman's role in Trent's life. He never mentioned her before. Of course, she could be the pot calling the kettle black, but she had mentioned Kevin to him.

"Rain? As in *Rain, rain, go away*?" Katrina laughed condescendingly.

Rayne's chest tightened and a weight pulled at her center of gravity, nearly causing her to double over in pain. Reaching down deep for the miniscule amount of dignity she had left, she smiled. "I, uh...I'll leave you two."

He didn't try to stop her when she fled down the hall and into the guest bathroom, and that hurt just as much as seeing the beautiful woman who appeared too comfortable in his bedroom.

It didn't make any sense. If Trent wasn't gay, then why hadn't he hit on her? Because he already had a girlfriend, Katrina. But that kiss, oh, that kiss was deeper and more sensual than one she'd ever experienced before. He wouldn't kiss her like that if he and Katrina were an item. Would he?

They'd spent countless hours walking, running, talking, laughing, going out to eat, doing fun stuff, and never once had he made a sexy remark, stared at her boobs—granted, they were tiny, but still—made a pass, kiss her other than on her cheek...he never, ever, ever hit on her and that truly hurt.

The kiss in his bedroom nearly melted her kneecaps. Thank God she had his shirt to hold onto or she would have fallen over. He kissed her like a man—not a gay man—who was attracted—at least a little—to a woman. He kissed her like he enjoyed it, the moans coming not only from her but from Trent as well. Obviously she misread those cues too.

As usual. Typical Rayne Wilde making something more of a situation than there was. This was why she was no good at relationships. In her book, a kiss like that meant happily ever after. Okay, maybe she had been a bit presumptuous in her interpretations in the past, but that kiss was...wow.

If Trent kissed every woman like that, then she

could understand why so many fell at his feet. Well, that and his scruffy good looks. And hot body. And killer smile. And funny personality. Other than that, Trent Kipson was a dog.

Rayne stared at her pale reflection in the bathroom mirror. *Get a grip, Rayne!* Her eyes weren't red; she hadn't had time to cry about it. And she definitely hadn't had time to figure out what *it* would be. Crying about an amazing kiss that would go nowhere? Crying over the fact that the man of her dreams was not gay and not interested in her? Crying about Hurricane Katrina who was most likely doing the nasty with her One True Love? No, no. Nothing to cry about at all.

Rayne splashed water on her face, plastered on a fake smile, and stepped out of the bathroom, shoulders back, head high. The first person she saw was Claire, and the sympathy in her eyes nearly made the waterworks start to flow. No, she was strong and had years of experience in handling rejection.

"Hey, sweetie," Claire said, rubbing a reassuring hand up her arm. "You okay?"

"Me? Of course." Rayne laughed. "That was quite a misunderstanding. I must have really wounded his ego. I'm really embarrassed. Oh well. No harm, no foul, right? So let me guess, you and Brian are married?"

Claire nodded.

"How did Brian take it? Me thinking he was gay?" Better to laugh at the situation than think about what it all meant.

A sly smile erupted from Claire's lips. "When it

was just about Trent, he thought it was hilarious. Couldn't stop laughing when he returned from the grocery store last night. When I pointed out that you must have thought he was Trent's boy toy…well, that wasn't so funny." Claire laughed.

If she hadn't been so coldly rejected five minutes ago by the love of her life, she too would view the situation as a little funny.

"There you are, babe," Kevin said as he set his empty beer bottle on the counter. "Hey, so, Curtis texted me about some arm wrestling tournament at Breakers. Grand prize is five hundred bucks. I've got this one nailed." He pulled up his shirtsleeve, flexed, and kissed the mountain peak on his bicep.

"Uh, yeah. Totally, Kev."

"Knew you'd understand. The bar's a few blocks from here. I'm gonna walk down, loosen up a little. You can come cheer me on when you're done here. You don't mind, do you?"

Aware of Brian's, and now Trent and Katrina's, presence behind her, she plastered on another fake smile. "Oh, gosh, Kev. This is a great opportunity. I don't want to miss a thing. I'll go with you." Opportunity, her ass. It was the perfect excuse to rush out of Trent's house before she lost all self-control.

She turned to everyone in the room, thanked them for a lovely time, and quickly headed out the door before anyone could object. Thankful that she had insisted on driving—more so because she knew Kevin would end up drinking himself stupid—Rayne slid behind the wheel of her car and fought back tears.

She pulled up to the curb in front of the bar. "I'm really not feeling well. Why don't you go in, have some fun and call me tomorrow. Let me know how it goes?"

"Yeah, sure thing, babe." He leaned over the console and kissed her on the lips. It felt like cold stone. Not the soft, warm, melt-in-your-mouth kisses that Trent gave her not long ago.

There was definitely no future in sight with Kevin; she'd break it to him easily. Turning thirty-five, which was old in the bodybuilding world, made him *think* he needed a wife and kids. Not that he desired them, but he thought it would be good for his image now that he was moving up in age. Four months ago she thought it sweet that he chose her to bear his children and take on his name, even though she had reservations about becoming Mrs. Kevin Magoo. She couldn't imagine the taunting he got in school. Maybe that was why he turned to weight lifting and bodybuilding. Their relationship never turned too serious, so she'd never know.

Yet she had been willing to marry the man, pop out monstrous-size babies, no doubt, and didn't know a thing about him. He didn't know nearly as much about her as Trent did. She never told Kevin about her childhood obesity. That would have been a sure turn-off. Maybe she'd wave that red flag under his nose if he came back around asking her to be Mrs. Babymaker Magoo.

Her gas tank and heart were both nearly empty. It sure wasn't the night she had anticipated. But what did she expect? Realizing she completely missed dinner, she pulled up to a drive-thru and ordered a cheeseburger and fries. The last time she'd done that she was one hundred pounds heavier and living a depressing life. When she got home she took two bites of the greasy burger, swiped three fries through a gallon of ketchup, and dumped the rest in the trash.

The sun would set in less than an hour and there were bound to be a bazillion drunks on the road, so she quickly changed into her running gear and ran the loop through the residential streets of Saco and through the beautiful old cemetery.

By the time she got home she was tired, hungry, sad, depressed, and extremely confused as she fell into her bed, sweaty clothes and all, and dreamed about the Love of her Life who was not, in fact, gay.

Chapter Four

Rayne

"Oh, honey. You know I love you and I don't ever beat around the bush, and I'm not gonna start now." Sage shook her head and sighed. "Give me the polish."

Rayne leaned down and handed over the bottle of *Heartbreak Hotel Red* and stuck her foot in Sage's lap. It had become their tradition during their unsuccessful hunt for love. Well, Rayne's hunt, Sage's avoidance. The dumpee got a pedicure while the other offered support. Sage preferred Ben & Jerry's. Rayne, not a big fan of sugar, would cry through a family size bag of extra-nacho cheese Doritos while Thyme would mow through chocolate cake.

She sucked the orange off her fingers. "I'm going to need a manicure too," she said around another mouthful of chips.

"Damn, I knew this would happen. He sounded too good to be true."

"That's why he was gay."

"He's not gay, though."

"I know and that totally sucks. Sage, the man can kiss. Holy shmoly, I would've taken him right then, right there. But then he apologized and said he only meant to prove a point…" Rayne hiccupped and let the tears fall.

Sage had heard the story four times already—the price of being the sister of a walked-over romantic—and scowled.

"I haven't decided if I like him or hate him for pulling back."

"What? Are you nuts?" Sage pointed the nail polish brush at Rayne. "He worked you over big time, Rayne. Don't do this to yourself. Cut the ties and be free. He made it clear he wasn't interested."

Rayne shook her head. "No, he was being honest. He said he wasn't interested in a relationship. A romantic one. We'll continue with our friendship and our adventures. It's my turn on Wednesday."

She hoped Trent wouldn't stop their weekly outings. It had gotten fun trying to one-up the other person's plans, and she knew she'd win this time.

"Honey, that's in two days. Do you really believe you're going to be over this and be able to maintain a friendly relationship? You could barely handle that when you thought he was gay."

"I know," she sighed, reaching for her glass of Chablis. "It's just…I really like him. And maybe this is what I need. A friend. I'm not going into this blind. I know there won't be a ring at the end of this relationship…well, I hope this relationship never ends. If it's a true friendship it will go on for years and years."

"Uh huh," Sage said skeptically. "And you, what? Are going to throw him a bachelor party when he finally settles down? Be his child's godmother? Come on, Raynie, you know this is too much. You gotta end this…this…whatever it is you two have."

Rayne studied her beautiful pedicure and smiled. "No. This time I'm stronger. I'm not following my heart. That, I've packed away. I'm following my head and keeping it screwed on straight. I'm friends with a hot guy who sleeps with other women and I don't care because I'm not looking for a relationship."

She searched the bottom of the Doritos bag and found nothing but smooshed-up chips. Rayne tipped up the bag and let the crumbs fall into her mouth and down her shirt.

What a freakin' mess.

***

Trent

Normally he would have called her the night before to confirm the meeting time, but he wasn't so sure Rayne wanted anything to do with him anymore. She never called or texted him after her abrupt departure on Sunday, and he didn't think she'd want to continue with their weekly adventures, not after his insensitive rebuff.

Trent stood in his kitchen in his boxers and

contemplated his choices—a) Call her and reassure her their friendship is really important to him. b) Leave her alone and never talk with her again. c) Call and apologize for being an ass and tell her that he'd like to take this further. All the way to his bed.

No, Option C couldn't happen. He knew a quick roll in the hay with Rayne would never be enough. After a few weekends, maybe even a couple months, they'd become bored with each other. Or rather, she'd get bored—he couldn't imagine growing tired of her—and either find someone else, or ask him for forever and ever. Neither of those options appealed to him.

Yeah, he was a head case.

Running his hands through his bedhead, he contemplated going for a run or letting off some steam in the bakery. His employees were used to him waltzing in on his day off. He glanced at the clock. Eight. The morning rush would be over and he could sulk and pound on dough for a while. Maybe get a head start on the Wilsons' wedding cake.

Just as he sat down at his kitchen table to sketch out another wedding cake design, the doorbell rang. Frustrated, expecting it to be Katrina—she had no neighborly boundaries—he growled, "Hang on!"

Not wanting to open the door all the way, as she'd see that as an open invitation to his life, he kept the chain on the door and opened it a few inches. "What?"

"Well, aren't we Mr. Grouchy Pants this morning," Rayne chirped.

He closed the door, unlatched the chain and

swung it open again. "Hey. Yeah, come in." She was beautiful. Her dark hair was pulled back in her trademark ponytail and she wore a bright blue Dri-fit shirt that somehow made her dark eyes glow. Her fitted pants—spandex? Yoga pants?—whatever they were called, he thanked God for inventing them. He didn't like feeling like a girl, but the effect she had on him was potent.

"Or should I say Mr. Grouchy Boxers?" she teased.

Trent looked down and swore. Any second now she would see how happy he was to see her.

"Yeah, um, I'm going to go throw on some clothes." He turned to leave, glancing over his shoulder. "Don't go anywhere."

She laughed, making him very grateful his front wasn't facing her. Yeah, he sure as hell was happy now.

***

Rayne

Rayne took a few minutes to regain her composure. The last thing she'd expected was a nearly naked Trent. She figured he'd make some excuse as to why he had to cancel their date.

No, not date. Adventure. Friends didn't go on dates.

Trent's living room didn't scream *bachelor* but it lacked the intimate knick-knacks most homes had. His mantel was nearly bare except for two framed photographs. One was of an adorable toothless

Faith, a drooling, smiling mess, and the other of Claire sandwiched between Trent and Brian, Faith swaddled in her lap.

He didn't say much about his childhood, only that his mother had abandoned him and Claire at a young age and his father died not long after. Trent had picked up the responsibility around the house and even sacrificed his college dreams to pay for Claire's schooling. The poor kids.

Although her childhood wasn't much better. Being the middle child had helped her master the position of peacemaker. Sage, being the oldest, had always been self-centered. That didn't bother Rayne. She figured it to be an oldest child trait, while Thyme carried the "baby of the family" traits. Sweet, adorable, able to get away with anything…the one everyone loved and took care of. The one who could do no wrong, but also lacked any sense of responsibility.

Sage and Thyme were as opposite as could be, which left Rayne as the middleman, always trying to make everyone happy. Once Sage turned fifteen and was capable of babysitting, their parents would take off for weeks on end, saying how important it was for spouses to have alone time.

Suzie and Neil Wilde were more into each other than their children. The spark between them never dimmed, never grew tiresome. To say the Wilde girls were neglected may be a bit harsh, but that's how Sage interpreted it. She had a perpetual chip on her shoulder and made the world center around herself. Rayne couldn't blame her. As the oldest, Sage felt the most rejected.

Their parents expected a lot from her and even though there was only a fifteen-month age difference between each girl, Sage had to grow up fast to make it in the Wilde house. There were times when their parents forgot to pick them up from school—which could be understandable if it happened on rare occasions, but it happened weekly.

Neil provided for his girls, barely. They lived in a two-bedroom ranch style home in the middle of nowhere and were fairly self-sufficient. Rayne's parents grew herbs, fruits, and vegetables, and raised the meat and milk they consumed from goats, chickens, and even pigs. Not much of red meat fans, the Wildes lived off their farm and rarely got into town. Not that there was much of a town. Parish Farm was a good twenty minutes northwest of Cornish, which wasn't much more than a general store and post office. During Sage's wild years, Rayne often covered for her, not that Suzie or Neil noticed when their eldest didn't make it home on a Friday night. As long as the girls didn't interfere with the farming or their parents' life, all was fine in the Wilde home.

Their parents had been—and still were—clueless when it came to parenting. Rayne often found herself defending her parents, chastising her sisters for misbehaving, and trying to instill a touch of family in the house.

Rayne picked up the photograph from Trent's mantel and smiled. The similarities between brother and sister were so striking they could pass as twins. His eyes were green to her blue, but the shape and brightness shone alike. As did their chiseled cheekbones. How the heck could she have believed Trent played for the other team? Thank God he didn't, although that made their relationship much more complex.

"Sorry it took me so long. The bakery called with a slight emergency."

"Oh, I'll let you go then." She put the photo back on the mantel and picked up her purse.

"No, no. I took care of it. Just a little mess up with next week's order. All is good." He smiled and she resisted the urge to reach out and stroke his freshly shaven face.

The five o'clock shadow, when he had it, made him appear like a rogue, while the clean-shaven face gave him an Abercrombie appearance. Both looks were devastating to her deserted libido.

"You said swimming…is this okay?"

She started with his feet, clad in leather flip-flops, and worked her way up his bare calves—not too hairy, and definitely muscled—to his long swim trunks. Navy blue with a white stripe down the side. Simple and masculine—nothing Hawaiian or flamboyant for this straight guy. Her eyes lingered on his abs. Abs she'd been fortunate enough to see a few minutes ago and would like to see again. And lick. Taste.

Stop that! Trent Kipson was one hundred percent off limits. For some reason he agreed to go out with her while dating the bimbo model next door, and she wouldn't look a gift horse in the mouth.

The t-shirt had seen better days, but it stretched so nicely across his wide shoulders that she didn't give it another thought. *Yummy.*

"Rayne?"

Darn. He caught her staring. But her eyes weren't done yet.

"Perfect. I mean fine. You look good. Fine. Yeah, I mean, we're just chilling and may go for a swim and—"

"Hey." Trent stepped closer and her heart did little flip-flops in her chest. *Breathe, breathe, breathe. Pretend he's gay!* "You okay? We can do this…thing another day."

"No! I mean…no. I'm fine. Just a little warm. Which is why this outing is going to be so much fun!" Plastering on her fake smile, Rayne grabbed his arm and hauled him out the door before the intimate feel of his apartment caused her to do something ridiculous like blurt out her love for him and tackle him to the floor. Rayne pointed to the canoe tied down to the top of her car. "We're going canoeing down the Saco River. Ever been?"

"Sort of, but not really. A bunch of buddies of mine got together after high school graduation. Packed a tent, about ten coolers. Nine of them held beer. One had some meat. Needless to say, we didn't do much canoeing. We camped out, met up with some girls, and…yeah, well. We didn't really canoe much."

His cheeks turned red. So deliciously sweet and adorable. Maybe she did have a sweet tooth after all.

***

Trent

She got too much pleasure out of torturing him, that was obvious. With Rayne sitting in the front of the canoe, her tanned and toned back to him, Trent was forced to stare and drool as they paddled down the shallow river. They passed many families and a few rowdy teenagers, but mostly their excursion was mellow. After an hour or so of lust-filled mind wandering, they paddled to a sandy cove.

"I'm hungry, so I bet you're starved."

Unfortunately, Rayne pulled a black dress thing over her turquoise bikini and reached down for the cooler.

"I've got it. Why don't you grab the bag?"

"Chauvinist," she muttered with a smile.

"No, a gentleman." He winked and hefted the cooler out of the canoe. "Damn, woman. What did you pack in here?"

"I know you have quite the appetite, so I packed a little of everything."

And by everything, she meant *everything*. Meat-filled subs, pasta salad, potato salad, fruit salad, granola bars, cheese and crackers, hummus, some other sort of healthy-looking stuff…the woman knew the way to a man's heart. Except she didn't pack any dessert.

And Trent had one hell of a sweet tooth. Staring at her glistening pink lips, he thought of a very suitable replacement for dessert. They sat on a blanket under a tree, ate, and talked about other items on their bucket list. For him, skydiving, parasailing, bungee jumping. She had more tame events: climbing the Eiffel Tower, walking through the Aztec ruins, hiking the Appalachian Trail. And of course, starting a family.

Yeah, he could totally see himself doing those things with her. Except the family part. They argued over their lists and laughed at each other's jokes. It was too damn bad he couldn't give Rayne what she desired.

"No cookies?"

"I didn't think you'd have room after all this."

"Hell, I thought you knew me better than that. I always have room for dessert."

"You just wait. One of these days all those snacks are going to catch up to you and you're going to be mistaken for Santa Claus," she teased.

"And to think I shaved this morning for you," he said as he rubbed his cheeks.

"I like the scruff."

Trent raised an eyebrow and studied her. She had no idea how sexy she was. Or that everything she said and did turned him on. "Really? Why is that?" He leaned back on his elbows and looked up at her. Tanned skin, hair that was meant to be splayed across his pillow, nervous chocolate-syrupy eyes. He itched to reach out and tuck the stray curl behind her ear, but he knew he wouldn't be able to stop there.

Rayne pulled her knees up to her chest, wrapping her arms around her legs, and stared out over the river. "You're a nice guy, Trent."

"Uh, oh. I've heard that one before." He chuckled, trying to lighten the moment.

She turned to face him and gave him a sad smile.

"I really like you and am glad we're still friends after…after my um, misunderstanding."

His heart softened. No, it turned into a melting puddle of ganache. If he was reading the signs right, she was interested. Very interested. That could either spell trouble or *hello sweet heaven*. But if he turned her down, that could ruin their friendship as well. Better to evade than to disappoint.

"Ten bucks says I'll beat you in."

Clearly confused, Rayne tilted her head.

"The water. I bet you're a toe dipper. Gotta get used to the water slowly. I'm a head diver. No holds barred for me. Think you have it in you?"

"Seriously?"

"Hell yeah."

Okay, maybe he read her wrong. He thought she was annoyed that he turned their conversation into something as ridiculous as a wager. While wondering if he should apologize for his insensitivity, she bolted up, stripped the black dress off, and ran into the river, diving under the water before he brought himself to his feet.

The devious brat.

The shallow water only reached her thighs—and oh, what a sight!—and dripped off her nearly naked body that glistened in the sun. She rested her hands on her hips and yelled, "You owe me ten bucks!"

He laughed and ran into the river, tackling her underwater with him.

"You cheat," he said as they came up for air.

"How so?"

"I never said *go*."

"Oh please." She splashed him. "You're such a

sore loser."

"Am not."

"Are too. Now let's pack up. We still have another hour or so until we reach the landing." Trent followed her, stopping to appreciate how her wet bathing suit molded to her butt, her long hair dripping water down her back into no-man's land. His gaze followed the drops as they disappeared under her suit, fantasizing about following the same path with his tongue. "Unless you'd rather swim for a bit. The shuttles come every thirty minutes, so it doesn't really matter what time we get there."

They'd get picked up by a van and shuttled back to her car ten miles up the river. Some people made a weekend of it, tenting out alongside the river. Him, Rayne, sleeping bag, tent. No, not a good idea. She wasn't a one-night-stand kind of girl and he didn't do commitment. He didn't do forever.

And Rayne Wilde was a forever kind of girl.

***

Rayne

"That was fun. You're a good sport. Now hand over my money." Rayne held out her palm to Trent as he unbuckled his seatbelt.

Picking up her hand, he turned it and brought her knuckles to his lips. "Will you take an IOU?"

Red alert! Red alert! She could either cave in to his sweet caress, accidentally lean into him, and bump her lips against his, or she could pull away and act pissed that he would not make good on his bet.

The latter won out.

"You suffered through six Zumba classes but you can't pay up ten dollars? Geesh. Never took you for a cheapskate. I'll have to tell Brian about this one," she teased.

"You are pure evil. I thought my good looks and charm would get me out of it." Trent scooted up in his seat and reached into his back pocket for his wallet. As he rifled through, counting out his bills, she peered over his arm and saw the ominous ring of a condom.

Of course he carried protection with him. Trent had women falling at his feet wherever he went. He oozed testosterone and sex. But not with her. No, he made it blatantly obvious he liked her as a friend. Apparently he liked the model-thin trampy types like Katrina. Well, if that was his taste, pooh to him!

"All I have are twenties. Do you want to owe me or want me to owe you?"

"Here's a deal. I need a cake for my parents' anniversary next week. I was planning on picking one up at the grocery store—"

Trent's dramatic gasp startled her. "I don't *ever* want to hear you talk like that again." He shook his head in disgust. "Do you know they order their frosting in bulk in cans? Who knows what chemicals they put into those things? Come to Sweet Spot. I'll hook you up with a cake. How big? What flavors? We can do a decadent chocolate ganache or a lighter lemon curd or—"

"Whoa. Down boy. We're talking about my

parents, Mr. and Mrs. Granola. They'd be fine with goat's milk on a bed of lettuce, but it's their fortieth. I thought a cake would be nice. Nothing big and fancy. It'll just be my sisters and Suzie and Neil. Nothing spectacular. They'd rather spend it without anyone around anyway, so it's going to be a short and sweet dinner. Well, maybe not so sweet. Sage will have a temper tantrum and be grumbling about something and Thyme will be late, if she remembers at all."

"And to think I felt left out not being invited."

Well that was an idea. Rayne had been known to bring men to their sporadic family dinners. She'd always wanted a big table full of friends and family to talk and laugh with over a meal. Make memories. Start traditions. If Neil, Suzie, Sage, and Thyme had their way, the Wildes would never see each other, so Rayne made it her mission to bring the family together when her parents were actually around. This year it coincided with her parents' anniversary.

Having a man with her distracted the family, gave them something to talk about, and took the pressure off Sage's stress and anxiety and Thyme's unwillingness to commit to…anything. Neil had a man to talk to and Rayne would talk to Suzie about herbs and new garden trends.

Maybe Trent would fit right in. He could talk recipes with her parents. They weren't big on sweets either—only organically fresh food for them—but she bet they could swap a few recipes.

"Actually, if you're not doing anything next Saturday night, you're more than welcome to come. Sage and Thyme will do most of the cooking at my folks' place in Parish Hill. Feel like an adventure? You can scratch it off your bucket list."

"It's not that bad, is it?"

"Oh, just you wait and see."

Chapter Five

Rayne

The cake wasn't ready when she stopped by Sweet Spot to pick it up. Instead, the nice woman behind the counter introduced herself as Marie, Brian's mother, and told her to go on back. Reluctantly Rayne pushed through the swinging doors and called out to Trent.

"Just in time." He wiped his hands on a towel and handed her a white apron. "Tie this on. You don't want to get your clothes messy."

Rayne looked down at her denim shorts and squinted. "Not really concerned about the wardrobe, Trent. I'm just picking up the cake. What did you come up with?"

"Nothing."

"Nothing? Well, okay. I don't really need it today. As long as it's ready when I leave tomorrow—"

"I'm not coming up with anything. You are. It's your parents. I'll help you with some ideas but I thought it would be pretty cool if you made the cake."

She snorted. "Me? I can't bake. Stir fry, grill, sure, but I don't do sweets. I've never even made cookies. Not even the kind you buy at the store with the dough in those tube things—"

Trent covered her mouth with his finger. "Shh, we don't talk about such things in the house of confections. That's blasphemy." He pulled his hand away and turned her so he could tie her apron. "I'll guide you. All you have to do is follow orders. You can do that, right?" He spun her around and yanked on her ponytail. Such a brotherly, friendly gesture.

She hated it.

"Sure. Whatever. Tell me what to do," she snarled.

"That's the spirit!" He gently chucked her chin with his knuckles and pushed her toward the sink. "First, wash up."

After listening to about fourteen thousand sugary combinations, she opted for a coconut cream cake with raspberry filling. Ever the model student, Rayne followed Trent's directions and measured, poured, stirred, sifted, whipped, and creamed. Her arms ached after an hour of baking.

"Why couldn't we use one of those big mixer things?" she asked after they put the cake in the oven and the filling in the fridge. "My arms are killing me from all that beating."

"Sounds to me like you need a new personal trainer," he teased.

"Bite me," she growled and watched his eyes darken. "You did this on purpose to torture me."

"Oh, stop being a baby and go wash the dishes."

"I don't know why I couldn't have given them one of the lovely cakes you have in the display case up front," she grumbled on her way to the sink. "I'll wash but you dry."

They worked together, her banging dishes around while he whistled and laughed at her grumpy mood. Only she wasn't grumpy about the upper body workout or dish duty. She wore her favorite red halter-top. The one that made her look like she had a C cup. It showed off her shoulders and dipped a bit in the back to reveal her shoulder blades. The daisy dukes weren't super short but she knew they did tremendous things to her booty. And Trent never let his eyes stray from her face. Maybe the man was gay and didn't know it yet.

She held back a snort. As if.

Rayne didn't always get hit on, not in regular clothes and with a naked face, but when she put a little makeup on—just a touch of mascara and some shiny lip gloss—like she did today, and spent a few extra minutes on her hair and wardrobe, she could turn a few heads.

And the only head she hoped to turn had no intention of looking her way. She'd give him until tomorrow, and if he didn't put the moves on her by the end of the night, she'd body tackle him to the floor.

***

Marianne Rice

Trent

"I deserve a freakin' award," Trent grumbled before he took a swig from his bottle of beer.

"No, you deserve a kick in the ass. I don't get why you don't throw on the infamous Kipson magic and charm her pants off." Brian laughed.

"I can't."

"Why the hell not? You like her, right? She's hot. She's funny. You two seem to have a lot in common. Are you afraid you'll fall in love or something?" Brian flipped the burgers on the grill and popped open another beer.

Trent grabbed a handful of chips, chewed, and contemplated how much he should tell his friend. "She's different than the women I date."

"No kidding," Brian laughed. "She has a brain and a personality."

Rolling his eyes, he bent to scoop up Faith, using her as a shield, and patted her back. "We're friends—"

"Friends that—"

"Don't you dare say it, man. Yeah, I like her. I respect her a hell of a lot too. She's had…relationship issues in the past."

"And you haven't?"

Trent sighed. "She tends to get emotionally attached pretty fast. Falls hard before the second date."

"And you're worried she'll fall in love with you?"

It did sound pretty arrogant when put that way, but she was the one who admitted to doing so.

"Yeah, something like that."

"And that would be a bad thing…why?"

Trent scowled. "I don't *do* love. I'd break her heart before the end of dinner."

"It seems to me," Brian said, taking Faith in his arms, "that you two have had dinner before. She in love with you already?"

That stopped him in his tracks. Damn. What if she was? He couldn't lead her on anymore. That wouldn't be fair. He'd use his upcoming trip to LA to put some distance between them and hopefully diffuse any romantic ideas she had in her head.

"Dude, stop the train. I can see the fear bubbling up inside you. Don't dump her now because you're afraid she may have feelings for you. Why don't you hop on board and go for a ride? See how she feels." Brian smirked.

Trent snatched the spatula and took the burgers off the grill. "Food's ready." He needed time to figure out what to do. One part of him—his lower half—definitely wanted to take Rayne for a test drive. But his head said other things. And his heart—damn, his heart never got involved—seemed to have a mind of its own. He needed some time to himself to figure out exactly what that organ was trying to tell him. Damn if it ever talked to him before.

***

Rayne

It wasn't like Trent was the first guy she ever

introduced to her family, but the other two men had been fiancés at the time. After a dinner with surly Sage and her parents' sickening lovey-dovey behavior, both fiancés had gone off running. Or maybe it was Rayne they ran from. If Kevin or Roger truly loved her, they would have gotten past her family's idiosyncrasies.

Granted, this time she wasn't introducing a fiancé, just a friend.

Unfortunately.

Rayne sighed and took one final peek in the mirror. Her lavender sundress showed off her sun-kissed skin, accentuating her curves in a flirty, not sexy manner. Sage would pick up on any sudden wardrobe changes. Rayne wasn't one for sexy dresses like Thyme.

Normally she kept her hair pulled back in a ponytail; she figured her hair needed a day off, so she wore it down. She may have had two fiancés in her wake but she'd never spent so much time prepping or caring how she looked. Trent seemed more interested in his stupid frosting and filling than he was in her. She lathered on her new coconut raspberry lotion that she picked up this morning in hopes of luring Trent to her sweet spot.

Tonight she'd wow him.

Hopefully.

***

Trent

It was damn near impossible to keep his hands

on the wheel and his tongue in his mouth. The woman smelled like she should be licked from head to toe. She was mouthwatering in her little, airy dress and tanned legs that stretched for miles. Thank God he was driving or he would have dived over the center console and taken her in the front seat.

Rayne seemed oblivious to her sex appeal. Which made her even more alluring. Trent reached over and cranked the air conditioner.

"Hot?"

He gulped and nodded. "Too cold?" His gaze skimmed her arms, searching for goosebumps.

"No. It feels good. The humidity is pretty gross today. I'm hoping I'll stay somewhat cool in this dress. I should have warned you my parents don't believe in air conditioning. The hotter the better, is their motto." She blushed and chewed on her lips.

Was she purposely trying to torture him? "Good to know." Yeah, he sounded stupid. She did this to him all the time, got him tongue-tied and sounding like a fifteen-year-old on his first date. He tried to block out her scent, her presence, and tuned in to the country music filling the car. Trent didn't want to think of running his hands through Rayne's hair and getting a rockin', so he pushed a button and changed to classic rock.

Nothing like a little AC/DC to kill the mood. If she noticed the tension in his body she didn't say anything. In fact, Rayne was unusually quiet. Nervous maybe? Had she brought any other men to meet her parents? Probably, considering she'd been engaged. Twice.

"So your parents...they know you're bringing...me?"

Rayne nodded. "I told my sisters I baked the cake and they threatened not to come. So I told them you helped. Which you did. A lot."

Interesting. So did they know who he was already? How exactly did she describe their friendship? If Sage was as direct and surly as Rayne had described her, he figured she'd tell him exactly what Rayne thought of him.

"And your parents?"

Rayne snorted. "I could have told them I was bringing the Portland Symphony Orchestra and they would have said, 'Great, honey.' They're so wrapped up in each other it doesn't really matter what my sisters and I do."

Instead of sounding angry like most daughters would, she sounded distant, sad. He reached out and patted her hand that rested on her thigh. She wrapped her fingers around his hand and squeezed.

They kept their fingers interlocked for the rest of the ride, neither saying a word. Other than his sister and Brian, Trent had never met a couple completely devoted to each other. Rayne had a warped version of love thrown in her face from birth, but the Wilde version was just as unhealthy as the Kipson one. Somewhere there had to be a happy medium. Brian and Claire had it, but they were lucky, a rare breed.

Trent had been able to shield Claire from most of the harsh realities of love, which was why she was a true believer now.

And poor Rayne. Even though she faced rejection every day of her life from her parents and crappy boyfriends, she still believed in happily ever after. The compassionate woman was a glutton for punishment.

"Their driveway is after the big maple tree." She pointed to the left. "Ready or not, welcome to the crazy Wilde house."

Trent laughed and squeezed her hand before letting go to grip the steering wheel. "I'll survive." He seriously doubted it.

Chapter Six

Rayne

"Nice job, Ray-Ray. He's gorgeous!" Thyme came up behind her and kissed her cheek.

Rayne rolled her eyes. "I told you. We're just friends."

"Why?" Thyme eyed him over her glass of red wine.

"Because he's a nice guy. I can talk to him about anything and we have fun together. We run, kayak, hike, and—"

"Have hot, sweaty monkey sex?"

"Thyme! Lower your voice. No, it's not like that. We're just friends."

Sage quirked an eyebrow and glared knowingly at her sister. "As if. You're hoping for the bended knee and ring tonight, aren't you? I warned you…"

Exasperated, Rayne sighed. She knew she'd get the third degree from her sister. "Friends, sis. Just friends, Rayne says," Sage said sarcastically.

Rayne allowed her gaze to drift to the main topic

of discussion. He seemed at ease with her parents. They kept their arms wrapped around one another but actually paid attention to Trent. Her mother even laughed at something he said.

The laugh carried over to the sisters, who were setting the table. "Wow. For a second there I thought Mom was going to let go of Dad. She must have fallen for your baker as well."

Rayne rolled her eyes at Sage and turned her back on her parents and her…friend. They had pulled two picnic tables together and draped them with white linen tablecloths. The bright colored Fiesta dishes and the bold flower arrangement Thyme made created a fun and romantic tablescape.

The night was still warm but Sage lit the tiki torches to keep away the bugs. "Dinner in five," Sage called out and sauntered—she never simply walked—into the house.

Trent looked over at Rayne and winked. She couldn't help but smile. And blush.

"Oh, honey. You're in love again, aren't you?" Thyme asked sympathetically. Apparently it was obvious to everyone but Trent. He still viewed her as a pal. Friendly pokes, hair tugs, light punches. Not something you do to someone you think of sexually. Or at least romantically.

Wishing she went for the slutty look and spent a little more time on hair and makeup, she sucked in her tummy and stuck out her chest a little more than necessary. Maybe she could work her assets to grab his attention. All she had to figure out was if he was a leg, butt, or chest guy.

***

Trent

Holy chest. He was getting hard while talking to Rayne's parents. Not that they'd notice. They were stuck on each other like Saran wrap, only faintly aware of other people in their vicinity. Trent had spent hours ogling Rayne's butt in the Zumba classes and couldn't help noticing her mile long legs as well, but her chest had always been kept trapped underneath the Lycra constraints of a sports bra. Let them out to play and...*damn*. The crème of the crème.

He wanted to lick her from...

"Trent?"

"Uh, yeah?"

Suzie Wilde eyed him suspiciously. "The girls said dinner is ready."

"Oh, yeah. Um, after you." He smiled and gestured for the happy couple to precede him. Hopefully they would shield their daughter's eyes from the impressive bulge in his pants.

The Wilde parents sat ridiculously close to one another at the picnic table while Thyme lowered herself next to her mother and Sage sat across from them. Rayne put a hand on his shoulder for support as she picked up her leg to straddle the bench. He got another glimpse of toned quad muscle. Swallowing deeply, he lowered himself between Rayne and Sage.

"Allow me, darling." Neil picked up the plate of grilled salmon and served his wife, seeming to know just how much she would eat.

"Oh, sweetie, thank you." She kissed his cheek and made adoring noises to her husband, completely ignoring her daughters.

Once the ladies served themselves, he dug in as well. "Wow, you girls can cook. This is delicious." Thyme smiled sweetly at Trent's compliment while Sage muttered, "Damn straight." Their parents only complimented each other, not their daughters, who planned, organized and cooked this fine feast.

"Thyme is amazing with herbs." *Go figure.* "She makes the best rosemary potatoes, doesn't she? Sage came up with the marinade for the salmon. She could give you some serious competition with your grill," Rayne said.

Trent smiled down at Rayne and whispered, "You never stayed to taste my grilling expertise, Ms. Wilde."

She stared into his eyes, blushed, and picked up her wine glass, drinking in a way that was very unladylike. He winked at Thyme, who stared back at him with amusement in her eyes before picking up her wine and hiding her grin in her glass.

The only one not affected by his charm was the serious sister to his right. Rayne didn't say too much about her older sister other than the fact that she liked to be in control of every situation. She seemed nice enough, but a bit too much like the Ice Queens he'd dated in the past. He supposed living with two parents who ceased to acknowledge your accomplishments or existence could do that to you. Somehow Rayne and Thyme escaped the negative, sour genes.

They ate in near silence, with only Rayne and Thyme talking frivolously, obviously trying to fill the dead air. He did his best at trying to work Neil and Suzie into the conversation, asking them how they met, but they told the story to each other, ignoring their family. Lost in their own world.

How could Rayne have such a high opinion of love and marriage after being emotionally rejected all her life?

"Who's ready for dessert?" Sage asked when she'd obviously had enough of her parents' neglect.

"Me!" Thyme cheered. "I can't wait to see what Rayne made! I still can't believe you baked. I'm assuming you had a pretty good teacher?"

"Yeah, he was all right. I've had better," she teased. Sage snorted and Rayne stilled. Blushing, she stammered, "I mean, I'm joking. I've never…um…well, it was my first time baking…I'll get the cake."

Trent stood up first. "I'll help. Your shoes aren't really meant for walking across a field."

She glanced down at her strappy sandals and bit her lip. "Don't trust me, Kipson?"

"Hey, I'm just looking out for the cake."

Getting up from the picnic table proved to be a struggle. He couldn't swing his leg over without knocking Sage with his back or kicking Rayne in the face. "Um, you may need to get up first."

Rayne swiveled around, putting her back to him—unfortunately—and swung her sexy legs over the bench. "Need a hand, big guy?" She held out her dainty hand and it was all he could do to not pull her down into his lap and show her exactly where he needed it.

"I'm good." He needed a little distance to tone down his libido. "You stay here. I'll grab it." He made his way to his SUV and opened the back to his built-in cooler, an essential when delivering cakes, pastries, and yeah, beer.

"I am man. Hear me roar," Sage said.

"Oh, quiet. He's just being gentlemanly," he heard Rayne scold her sister.

To say her sisters were impressed with the cake would be an understatement. Even Sage aww'd and rubbed Rayne's arm. "That's beautiful, Ray-Ray."

"You did that all by yourself?" Thyme asked.

"Well, no. Trent helped. You know me. I've never even baked a batch of cookies before. Anyway, you should see Trent's bakery. The cakes he decorates are gorgeous. Granted, I've only seen the three that were in the case that day…"

"Oh, easy. This masterpiece was completely Rayne. I stood by and told her what to do, but she baked the cake, made the frosting, and piped the roses. She's a natural." He set the cake in the middle of the table and stepped back so everyone could admire Rayne's masterpiece.

The tender smile she gave him made him sweat around the collar. *Hell, what am I getting myself into?* It was like he was trying to woo her instead of scare her off. His mouth kept firing off boyfriendish crap.

"I take back all the nasty things I said about you, baker boy. Anyone who can convince my sister to step foot into sugar land and turn out a product like this, deserves a…kiss."

Before he could stop her, Sage placed her hands on either side of his cheeks and planted a loud kiss square on his lips. He stood frozen, arms stiff at his side. *Shit.* Had he sent signals to the wrong sister? Sage pinched his cheek before slapping it lightly. "Don't worry, baker boy, I know you only have eyes for Ray-Ray. If you get bored with her, give me a call," she whispered in his ear.

"I'm going to cut the cake," Rayne said loudly, making her annoyance with her sister clear.

"Yes, cut the cake. It looks delicious." That was the nicest compliment Rayne's mother said all night. Trent wanted to sample Rayne's cake—and her mouth—and get the hell out of here. Fast.

***

Rayne

"I'm sorry. So, so sorry. I'm devoted to my family but we're pretty dysfunctional," Rayne said as soon as Trent slid behind the wheel.

"No apology necessary. What family isn't a little dysfunctional?"

"Oh, God, Trent. I didn't mean…I mean…your mom—"

"Rayne. Seriously. I'm fine. Don't even think about it."

She wanted to curl up and die. So much for seducing him. So much for convincing him to throw caution to the wind and give her a chance. Give a relationship a chance. Oh, and her sister. Boy, was she going to give Sage a piece of her mind in the morning. How dare she humiliate Rayne in front of Trent? Rayne sucked at seduction, but Sage sure knew how to work it.

And she was so Trent's type. Just like Katrina. Crap. Katrina. Who the heck did Rayne think she was, trying to seduce—ha! If she could call wearing a simple sundress seducing—a man who was incredibly out of her league and into women more like her older sister? Maybe she should hook them up.

No, Sage would eat him alive. Trent seemed like the kind of guy who liked that, or could at least handle it. Sweet was so not his style. He made that clear from day one. And day forty-two. His kiss was simply to prove a point. Not gay. But not interested.

Rayne stared out her window into the black night. At least traveling lightless, windy back roads would keep her face hidden from Trent.

"You're awfully quiet."

"Just tired. Thanks for coming tonight. Sorry it was so…awkward."

He didn't say anything, which was worse than trying to sound nonchalant. It was the first time they sat in uncomfortable silence. Normally they chatted freely and the few times they were quiet, it was still comfortable. Not tonight.

Forty minutes later, he pulled into her lot. As he got out and rounded the hood to her front door, she thought about what to say to him. There really was no way to make the night less awkward, so being forthcoming was her best bet. Biting her lip as he placed his hand on her lower back and escorted her to her apartment door, she breathed in and out slowly.

"You seem tense. Sure you're all right?" he asked as she got out her key to open her front door.

Now or never, baby.

Turning in the doorway, keeping Trent in the hall, she stared at his chest and blurted it out quickly. "No, I'm not all right. I like you. Like you a lot. You don't do relationships and I do. I'm willing to bypass my usual pattern, which hasn't been working for me anyway, and give your method a try. That is, if you're interested. Unless you're busy with your neighbor. Then never mind. I'm not looking for a relationship, just meaningless sex. Well, no, sex with you wouldn't be meaningless, but I promise not to fall in love with you. Sex doesn't make me fall in love, anyway. It's the relationship part and we won't do that. We'll just be friends. And we'll...you know. Or not. If not, we can still be friends and do fun stuff. Just not...that kind of fun stuff. " She gestured with her hands, let out a big breath and finally made eye contact. "Think about it. Get back to me. Good night." Rayne closed the door and locked it, then slithered down to the floor and burst into tears.

Chapter Seven

Rayne

"You did not!"

"Did too."

"And he didn't say anything?"

"Sage, I didn't give the man a chance. I slammed the door in his face, cried my eyes out, and called you."

"He didn't knock on the door? Break it down? Sweep you off your feet and screw you senseless?"

"Sage!"

"Damn. Is the guy like Fifty Shades or something?"

"Um, bad analogy. Fifty Shades is all about sex. This guy doesn't want it."

"With you. Oh, ouch. I didn't mean it that way. I mean, you told me he dripped sex. That he doesn't do relationships, just sex. Isn't that why you said what you said?"

"Yeah, except he doesn't want to have sex with me."

"You don't know that."

Rayne rolled over in her bed, hugging her pillow tight and switched her phone to speaker. "Yeah, I know that. He made it clear on the Fourth, remember?" She sure couldn't forget. That kiss lingered for hours. It's all she'd thought about for days. The reason she gave him an indecent proposal. With her past relationships, there had never been the strong chemistry, the tug at her heart, the desire to strip down naked and pounce on a man. She'd been searching for kind and nice and father material, not sex. Even Kevin with his bulging biceps, quads so big he could crush a guy between them, hadn't turned her on like Trent. Underneath Kevin's muscle there was a kind man. Not too smart, but a nice enough guy before he cheated. Hot sex was not part of the package she'd been looking for. Until now.

If Trent's lips could work that kind of magic, what could his hands do? The rest of his body? God, she desired him in the worst way. But she also had so much fun with him. He was perfect relationship material, he just didn't know it. And, yeah, she kind of lied to him. She was already head-over-heels in love with him. And he liked her a lot. That she knew. All she had to do was convince him to take their relationship to a sexual level and ta-da! Relationship in disguise.

Yeah, right. Who the hell was she kidding?

***

Trent

Trent stood outside her apartment for hours. Or at least if felt like it. She spooked the shit out of him. Sex? Rayne Wilde wanted to have sex with him? No-strings sex? And he was standing outside her door contemplating it like a freakin' idiot? What the hell was there to contemplate?

Everything.

Trent was no fool. It was a relationship that she was after, and she thought having sex with him would change his mind. He shook his head in disbelief and dragged his feet—and his aching groin—to his SUV. Sex with Rayne was not something to rush into.

Hell, he'd known the woman for two months. Longer than any woman he'd dated in the past. And that was why he couldn't jump into her bed. He had to be sure. They'd talk about it in a few days when she had time to come down from her disappointing visit with her parents.

And if he did this, if he did have sex with Rayne, he'd have to be straight-up honest. More honest than he'd ever been with any other woman. Damn. How did his life turn so complex?

***

Rayne

Normally Rayne didn't answer her iPhone while she was running, but she'd been waiting for a call from Trent for three days. She slowed and glanced at the number. Not him, but close enough.

"Hey, Claire."

"Rayne! How are you? I'm sorry we didn't get to spend much time together on the Fourth. I'm hoping you'll come up to the lake with me on Saturday? Stay the weekend?"

"Um, I don't know. I have to teach a class in the morning…"

"I wasn't planning on leaving until ten or so. I'd like to drive up during Faith's morning nap. Does that work for you? A day on the lake, floating or boating, whatever you prefer. I don't know about you but I could really use some girl time."

Girl time. Yeah, that did sound good. And no Trent. Yeah. She could do that.

"Sounds wonderful. Should I meet you at your place?"

"That would be great!"

"What can I bring?"

"Whatever your drink of choice is and maybe some snacks? I've got the fridge pretty well stocked. Brian and I were up last weekend opening up the camp. A little later than usual, which seems to be my life now with Faith." She laughed.

"Sure. Let me know if you need anything else."

They chatted for a few minutes before hanging up. It wasn't the person she had hoped to spend the weekend with, but maybe a few days with Trent's sister would give her some insight on him. A girls' weekend. Just what she needed.

"Oh, this is beautiful, Claire," Rayne said as they pulled into a small dirt driveway on Saturday afternoon. A cluster of large pines surrounded the

A-frame camp, and the grassy backyard was wide open, leading to a long dock where a boat bobbed up and down against the small waves.

"Thanks. It's been in Brian's family for years. We live the closest, so we've sort of accepted responsibility of opening and closing, but that also means we get to use it more often." Claire smiled as she unhitched the infant carrier from the backseat of her Tahoe.

"Where does Brian's family live?"

"You've met his mom, Marie. She lives outside of Portland, but since Brian's dad passed away a few years ago she only comes to camp for family gatherings. His brother married a few years ago and they moved to Texas. His other brother is in D.C. and he has aunts, uncles, and cousins scattered around the Midwest who make it out here every so often."

"That's nice," Rayne said as she unloaded a cooler from the back.

"Come inside. I'll show you around."

Claire led her into the small kitchen. The refrigerator and stove looked like they were at least fifty years old but they fit in the barely-accessible space.

"Not a lot of counter space, but we manage."

The kitchen, eating area, and living room were all open to each other. The walls were covered in dark brown clapboard and decked out with trophy fish and family photos. She'd have to check those out later.

"Here's the bathroom." The door opened to a tight space just large enough for a toilet, sink, and super-snug shower. "Brian and I usually sleep in the loft because it's more open and has a great view of the lake, but we'll take this back bedroom in case Faith wakes up in the middle of the night." Claire shifted the baby to her right hip.

Huh?

"Trent will sleep wherever. The couch, the other bunk in the loft, or…"

Oh no! "Trent's coming?" she whispered.

"Yeah, the boys are coming tonight after Bri's shift. We'll get some girl time in today and tomorrow morning while they're out fishing. Actually, now that I have you to keep me company, Brian will probably try talking Trent into going out fishing tonight as well."

"Oh."

"Rayne, is everything all right? I thought you two had smoothed things over since the Fourth."

Claire obviously had no idea about the indecent proposal she laid on Trent last week or the fact that he hadn't talked to her since.

"It's just that…well, Trent and I aren't really talking anymore."

"Oh dear God." Claire laid out a quilt on the living room floor and set Faith down with some toys. "What has that ass done now?" She tugged Rayne over to the sofa and gently pushed on her shoulders. "Do we need drinks for this conversation? Yes, by the look on your face, we do. I'll give the baby a bottle when she's hungry, so I can have one drink. White or red? Or something harder?" Claire bustled to the fridge.

"White's good." God, what should she tell

Claire? The woman was sweet, adorable, and definitely good friend material, but she was also Trent's sister. A little awkward.

"Here. Drink first, then spill. Don't hold back. Just because we share blood doesn't mean I'll take Trent's side. I have a feeling I'm going to side with you. I like you a lot more than him right now."

"You do? Why? What else has he done?"

"You look like you'd rather swim across this lake than face him. The snide ass. And he never said anything when I told him about this weekend."

"You told him I'd be here?"

"Of course. He thought it was a great idea."

"He did?" Maybe he was too afraid to face her alone and he felt he could hold off her sexual prowess with others around. *Great. No action for me.*

"So, spill."

Oh, yes. How much should she say? "Well, he didn't actually *do* anything. That's sort of the problem. I told him I was interested in being more than friends, and he hasn't talked to me since. It's been a week."

"What did he say when you told him this?"

"Nothing."

"Nothing?"

"I sort of closed the door in his face and didn't give him time to react." Rayne went through the story again, explaining her embarrassing proposition.

"Hmm," Claire said, tapping her lip with her finger. "Probably a good thing. If he needs time to think about this and didn't quickly pounce in your bed, I'd say that's an improvement."

"I'd say it's rejection," Rayne mumbled and finished off her wine.

Claire quickly refilled the glass. "No, this is good. He likes you. Respects you. He's not going to use you like he has other women."

Feeling a bit braver after the second glass of wine she accidentally guzzled, Rayne confessed some more. "I wouldn't mind if he used me."

Claire snorted her wine and covered her mouth as she laughed. "Oh, you're in deep."

"I know. That's the problem. I do commitment, he does not. He was quite clear on that from the beginning. I know it has to do with your mother and father…sorry."

"Oh, don't apologize to me or for Trent. We grew up in the same house and had the same crappy mother and father. I chose to learn from them and their mistakes and look at me." She beamed. "I have an amazing husband and the most wonderful daughter in the world." She turned her tender gaze toward Faith, who chewed on her toes and cooed. "So perfect. Trent can take his sour attitude and shove it. He probably believes all relationships are doomed. And if he does, well, then Brian and I take that personally."

"He's only said wonderful things about the two of you. He sees you as the exception to the rule. He doesn't say much about your parents or his childhood. All I know is it has caused him a lot of pain."

Claire sighed and tucked her feet under her legs. "Yeah. His childhood pretty much sucked. He did everything possible to please our dad. Once he hit junior high, he started hanging around with some pretty tough kids. Got into a lot of fights but Dad didn't seem to care. All Dad talked about was Mom. He'd take off for days, weeks actually, in search of her, and Trent had to take care of me."

"Did your father ever find your mom? Did she ever give any reasons for abandoning you?"

"Yeah. In a nutshell, she said we cramped her style. I was pretty young when she left us and never had much of a relationship with her anyway, so I didn't miss her. Trent spoiled me and took care of me. I grew up believing that was normal. I don't think he ever loved or missed our mom. His anger is more selfless. He wanted *me* to have a mom. And he wanted a dad to notice him. I guess that's why he turned into an overprotective brother."

"He loves you a lot. I always wanted a brother, but Sage inherited that role. She meddles in my and Thyme's business and scares the boys away." Like last week when she hit on Trent. Rayne was used to her sister doing things like that and trusted Sage completely.

Claire laughed. "I'd like to meet her. You'll have to invite your sisters up next time."

"I'd like that." Only if there was a next time. It would all depend on Trent's decision.

"Well, my brother is an ignorant ass but I do love him dearly. I hope he can let go of the past and not ruin things with you. Let's start on lunch and finish off that bottle of wine. I have a feeling you're going to want to be nice and buzzed when my idiot brother shows up."

Oh, she loved Trent. And his sister too.

Two hours later, the idiot brother gave Rayne a shy smile and a quick, "Hey," and continued unloading his SUV. So much for keeping things normal or falling at her feet. She'd settle for either. Preferably the latter.

Of course her shy, *"How's it going?"* didn't inspire any titillating conversation either. "Can I give you a hand?"

He barely made eye contact before sticking his head in the back of his vehicle. "Sure. I've got some groceries in the back seat." So much for a brush of his arm against her chest as he passed her something from the trunk. No, she'd schlep to the front of the vehicle and carry the damned bags. Ripping open the car door a little more forcibly than necessary, she snatched up the three reusable bags—*he cares about the environment! Gah! One more thing to drool over!*—and used her hip to close the door.

She took only two steps before a tree root totally jumped in front of her, causing her to trip and drop one of the ridiculously heavy bags.

Umph.

"Whoa. Quite the digger. You okay?" Trent knelt down and picked up the bottle of maple syrup and pancake mix that fell from the bag.

"Uh, yeah. Sure fine. Just sort of…you know, tripped. Didn't see that one coming." *Damn fourth glass of wine!* He didn't offer her a hand or help her to her feet, not that she would have allowed him to anyway. Attempting to keep—or regain—her dignity, Rayne brushed off the pine needles on her knees, snatched the bag Trent reloaded, and marched into the cabin.

Walking in on Brian and Claire playing tonsil hockey in the kitchen was not what she needed to see, but she didn't dislike the couple for their obvious signs of affection. It actually made her soften inside and whimsical for the HEA—The Happily Ever After that would probably never come.

Rayne cleared her throat but they seemed not to have heard her.

"God! Get a room!" Trent hollered from behind her.

That seemed to goad Brian even more. He pulled his wife in closer and dipped her back. Claire shrieked, which startled Faith, who then started crying.

"Trent!" Claire scolded her brother.

"Hey, don't blame me. You're the one who scared the poor kid. She's probably scarred for life. I know I am after seeing those pathetic moves," he teased Brian.

"Dude. I've got the magic down—"

"Brian Robert Smart! You shut your mouth right now!"

Trent barked out a laugh that was quickly interrupted.

"Trent Owen Kipson, if you know what's good for you you'll bite your tongue as well. You boys are stupid and immature," Claire said, rolling her eyes and fighting a grin. "Now, who's ready to go tubing?"

Claire insisted on driving while Trent put his life

jacket on and jumped out to the oversized tube. Rayne was comfortable holding Faith, who was cocooned in a life jacket as well, and sat up front. Brian let out the line as Claire gunned the engine.

"Geesh, Claire. Go easy."

"Easy, my butt," she grumbled, barely loud enough for Rayne to hear her. Rayne shielded the baby's eyes from the wind and turned to watch the man of her dreams hold on for dear life. Claire didn't slow the boat down as she weaved in and around, making waves in their wake. Trent's body was taking a beating every time the tube jolted over another crest, but his muscular shoulders and forearms held on.

It became too obvious to Rayne that Claire was being rough on Trent for her benefit, and she gave her new friend a knowing smile. She finally slowed the boat when Trent fell off.

"You're crazy, Claire. Payback's a bitch. Your turn." Trent smiled as he climbed up the ladder and dried off with the towel Brian handed him.

"As if. Rayne and I are going together. One of you will need to hold the baby." She stood and held out her hand to Rayne. "You said you wanted a turn, right?"

"Yeah, but you can go first."

Brian put a hand on her shoulder and whispered loudly in her ear. "My wife thinks if you're on the tube with her, Kipson won't retaliate. You gotta go with her or risk my poor daughter losing her mother at such a young age."

"Oh, well, for Faith then." She patted Brian's hand and winked at Claire. Rayne didn't look at

Trent but could feel his gaze on her as she pulled off her cover-up and stood in her turquoise bikini. *See what you're missing?* She heard his breath hitch and her lady parts started quivering.

Their tubing adventure was fun and nowhere near as death-defying as Trent's. Rayne accepted Trent's hand as she climbed up the ladder and delayed wrapping herself in the large towel. She wiped down her face, hair, arms and lastly, her legs, knowing she was putting on a show and enjoying watching Trent squirm. He'd shifted his body a dozen times in less than a minute before pulling a towel over his lap.

"Damn, woman. Put this on already." Trent shoved her cover-up at her and looked away. Brian started to laugh but stopped when Claire jabbed him in the ribs with her elbow.

Rayne refused to acknowledge Trent and sat up front, pulling her knees into her chest and wrapping her arms around them, facing the lake instead of the sexy man with beautiful green eyes she continued to get lost in. The lake was so calming, so peaceful, even with the occasional jet ski or water-skier passing by them.

"Some hot-shot football player has a place in the cove over there." Claire pointed to the opposite side of the lake. "Maybe tomorrow we'll sneak up and try to get a peek at him."

The men talked football while Rayne's mind worked like a hamster on its wheel, churning and churning but never going anywhere. Her relationship with Trent had obviously changed, whether she or he wanted it to. And it was all her fault. No more walking on eggshells. They needed to talk.

Chapter Eight

Trent

"Seriously. I don't think I'll ever eat again." Trent pushed his chair back and stretched out his legs, cautious not to rub them against Rayne's. "That was awesome, sis."

"Thank you. You boys are on dish patrol, since we cooked."

"I barely did anything, Claire. I don't mind helping." Rayne shot up from the table and began clearing the dishes. She'd been on edge the entire day, not that Trent expected anything else. He had an unfamiliar urge to draw her in his arms and comfort her, to tell her it was okay, that she shouldn't be embarrassed about her proposition. Seriously? No-strings sex? With Rayne? It was like he died and went to heaven.

Any other woman. Any other day.

No. No other woman would do. Not today, not tomorrow, not…well, Trent would be in California soon. The network had asked for one more session with him before finalizing the contract. With so many execs off for the summer, he'd have to wait until the fall before making anything official, but he could see the six figures on his checks. The glamorous life. Living out of posh hotels, having interns do all the prep and cleaning so he could focus on the baking and decorating and sampling. He'd be able to pay off Claire's medical school bills by Christmas and start a trust fund for his niece.

"I don't mind doing the dishes. You girls can go outside by the fire pit if you want. You suck at washing dishes." He tossed Brian a towel and filled up the tiny sink with water. "You can dry."

The women chose to stay inside, sitting on the floor and sipping wine while making baby noises to Faith. Having a family was never high on his list. Hell, it never made the list. He tried his best to shield Claire from the destruction their mother and father caused. Thankfully she was young and had a serious case of hero-worship when it came to Trent, so she seemed to be unaware of the abuse and neglect from both their parents. Too young to remember Sonya, Claire never realized a mother figure was even missing from their family.

Sonya Meadows—she refused to take her husband's name, saying it made her feel trapped—was never present anyway, so when she took off when Trent was eight and Claire six it wasn't like she left a big, empty hole to fill. Sonya liked to socialize, hang out with her friends sans husband and kids, and have a good time.

Children tended to interfere with her life and so, after eight years of being a "mom," she decided to get as far away as possible from the people who gave her that title. Over twenty years later and they had never heard from their mother again. No rumors, no whispers of her whereabouts. She had told Michael she was done with this life and never looked back once.

It wasn't like Sonya introduced her friends to her husband or children. She had a separate life, one that was much more enjoyable than being a wife or a mother.

And Michael Kipson was just as bad. He was obsessed with his wife to the point where he neglected his children and himself. Her blatant rejection turned him into a bitter drunk of a man. Since his father was too depressed to clean or maintain the house, Trent was forced into a leadership position in the household at the age of eight. If he and Claire wanted to eat, they had to fend for themselves.

Their father worked in a plant and brought home a paycheck each week. He paid the bills and usually remembered to go to the grocery store. By the time Trent was sixteen and had his license, all responsibilities fell on his shoulders—paying the bills, grocery shopping, making all the meals, chauffeuring Claire and keeping on top of their homework.

When his father's alarm didn't stop going off one morning, Trent figured his father took off during the night leaving Trent and Claire orphaned. Again. But it was worse. Michael Kipson lay in his bed, eyes closed, not a muscle moving.

His heart had stopped beating in his sleep. At

eighteen, Trent met with the funeral home and made all the arrangements. He didn't go to Johnson and Wales in Rhode Island that fall. Instead he went to community college and studied business so he could stay home and be his sister's guardian.

When she graduated from high school and went off to Tufts in Boston on a decent scholarship, Trent continued his education at the community college and took culinary classes. Not the same as the culinary school in Rhode Island or the one in New York he had hoped to transfer to after his sophomore year, but he was grateful his sister got to pursue her dreams.

When they were finished with the dishes, Brian tossed the wet towel on the counter and picked up a deck of cards. "How…how about a game of strip poker?" Claire snorted and Rayne looked like a deer in the headlights. Trent almost laughed.

"Let's stick with crazy eights, Magic Mike." Claire got up and kissed her husband. "Thanks for doing the dishes."

"You can repay me later." He kissed her loudly, earning another groan from Trent.

"Seriously, get a room."

"You got it, dude. Watch my kid. Be back…" He picked up Claire and flipped her over his shoulder, "in an hour."

"Put me down, Brian!" Claire pounded on his back and he slapped her behind.

"I will, once we make it to the bed. We have a babysitter. I'm not wasting it hanging out with your brother." He carried her down the short hallway and closed the bedroom door behind him.

Awkward. His sister and her husband were having sex fifteen feet away. And even more awkward was the silence between Rayne and him. Silence he didn't want filled with moans from down the hall.

"How about we take Faith for a walk?"

"Great idea." Rayne jumped up and scooped the baby in her arms. "The stroller is in the back of the van."

They walked in silence, enjoying the sunset, the only sound coming from the stroller wheels on the dirt road. This was his chance to finally talk to Rayne about the proverbial elephant that had been warping their relationship for the past week.

"So, about…last week." *Great opening, Kipson!* He threw the bone, hoping Rayne would chew on it, retract what she said, and laugh at her foolishness, but also praying she wouldn't. Trent noticed her knuckles tighten on the stroller, her lips quirk as she chewed the inside of her cheek, but she didn't say anything. "So, you were serious?" The quick glare she gave him answered that question.

Exasperated, Trent ran his hands up and down his face. "You've really got me confused, Rayne. I don't know what to do."

"What are your options?"

"What?"

"You don't know what to do? What are you weighing out in your mind? Pros and cons. Lay them on the table for me."

"That's easy. Pro—I get to have sex with you. Con—I have sex with you."

"Oh, I see."

"Do you?"

Rayne sighed. "No, actually I don't. I suppose sex as a pro is a compliment, but why is it also a con?"

"It just is."

He hoped she'd argue more, push him. She didn't. She continued pushing the stroller down the camp roads and turned left, heading back to the cabin. The night sky was bright, thanks to a nearly full moon, and he expected they had been gone long enough for Brian to get his rocks off, but he and Rayne still hadn't solved anything.

"Sex with you would be complicated, and I don't do complicated. You know that."

She stopped the stroller and turned to face him. The reflection of the moon over the water created dancing little moonbeams across her face, making her eyes shine. "I'm really sorry, Trent. I know I messed up our…friendship. Please just ignore what I said. It was a whim. A stupid one. I was upset with my parents and went a little crazy. I totally get why it wouldn't work and I'm okay with it too. I hope my brief bout of stupidity won't ruin our friendship." She gave him a friendly hug, patted him on the back, and released him before he had time to evaluate the platonic touch.

He had to jog a few paces to catch up with her and the stroller. What was that about? Did she just reject him? It was all too…easy. She gave up without a fight. Apparently she thought sex with him wasn't worth fighting for.

But did he feel the same?

Rayne

The following morning Rayne tried extra hard to be pleasant with Trent—but not so hard that he would pick up on her forced smiles. No more eggshells. Back to walking normally around him. Or possibly swimming.

"Hey, feel like a race?"

Trent eyed her suspiciously over his coffee. "What kind?"

"Swimming. Out to the little island and back." She nodded toward the island about five hundred feet from shore.

"Really? Have you ever swum that far before?"

"Please. Swimming is more about endurance than strength. That's where I've got you. You up for the challenge?" Before he could accept or deny her challenge, she ran out of the cabin, stripping her cover-up off at the same time. She didn't need to peek over her shoulder to know he'd followed her out. His testosterone filled the air, circling around her, and stirring the forgotten land between her legs. "That's what I thought. Need time to stretch, old man?" Rayne stopped when she got to the water's edge and turned to face him.

"Oh." Trent laughed. "Taunting me now? I've seen your competitive side but never so nasty." The grin on his face told her he didn't mind the insult.

"I was doing nothing of the sort," she teased and crisscrossed her arms back and forth, warming up her shoulders. "Stretching is crucial before any workout. Didn't you learn anything during the time you took my Zumba class?"

"I didn't learn what a smartass you were until later."

Rayne did twenty jumping jacks and a few lunges and watched with a secret smile as Trent worked to keep his gaze on her face and off her bouncing chest. She meant to taunt him, but he was doing an excellent job of teasing her by flexing his muscles. When he ripped his shirt off, exposing fine pectoral muscles and tanned, taut skin, she nearly hyperventilated. Yesterday his practically hairless chest was hidden under a life jacket, but today it was exposed and just begging to be touched.

Rubbing her hands together to keep them busy, she called over her shoulder, "Last one back's a rotten egg!" while running down the dock and diving into the cool water. She was underwater, kicking rapidly, when she heard the splash close behind. Game face on, Rayne worked her best Michael Phelps and freestyled it toward the island. It didn't seem too far away when standing on the edge of the dock, but from the fish-eye view in the water, it felt like three football fields stood between her and dry land. No sooner was she mentally kicking herself in the shins than she saw—or rather felt—Trent swim by her.

Never one to give up a fight, Rayne used all her Zen to focus on her breathing and her strokes. If he wanted to sprint early on and tire out before he made it to the island, good for him. She had enough sense to keep a steady pace, monitoring her heartbeat and taking big gulps of air.

Sweet on You

Trent started to slow as he neared the island, and Rayne swam up behind him, then crawled up the sandy shoreline next to him.

"We can take a breather before heading back," Trent said between gulps of air. Water dripped rapidly from his short hair and made sexy little streams down his cheek, neck, and chest. She forced her gaze to stop following the path once it hit his abs. What was a girl to do? His chest continued to contract rapidly, his breath still short and shallow.

"If you need the handicap, I'll give it to you. I'm heading back." She turned to dive in again, but Trent's hand wrapped around her bicep.

"Easy, babe. You're going to cramp up and I'm in no condition to save you. We both could use a rest. Besides, we never determined the prize."

"Huh. I was just doing this for bragging rights but if you feel like a wager, I'm in. Now let's see…what did you lose last time? Oh, yes, ten bucks and Zumba class. Care to try ballet next? I think you'd look really hot in a tutu."

"Har, har, har. I'll go easy on you. Loser cooks the winner a dinner of their choice."

"Sure. That's a win-win situation for me. I win, I get a great meal. You win, I get to poison you with my crappy cooking skills."

"I doubt you're that bad. Deal?" He held out his hand and she shook it, ignoring the jolts of electricity that shot up her arm and caused goosebumps to break out over her body.

"Deal." She took off running through the shin-high water until it was deep enough for her to dive. Trent passed her once again, but not before shoving her shoulder and laughing as she fell face first into the water. "Jackass!" she yelled when she came up for air.

The swim back seemed to take forever. When they eventually made it to the dock, Brian and Claire were cheering them on from the shore.

"Come on, Rayne! Push it! You're nearly neck and neck!"

"Dude! You're gonna get your ass kicked by a girl." Brian laughed but stopped when Claire slapped him on the arm.

Trent turned back to see his competition, and she seized the opportunity to pounce on his back, shoving him under the water and swimming by, beating him by two strokes.

"Woo hoo!" Claire shouted and jumped up and down. "You go girl!" She gave Rayne a high-five and then handed her a towel.

Too exhausted to talk, she settled for a wide-mouthed grin and dried off. Her limbs ached as if she'd run a 10K marathon.

"You...cheat...ed," Trent huffed.

"Sore loser."

He scowled and grabbed the towel from her since no one bothered to bring him out one. The way he scorched her with his eyes made her feel naked and vulnerable standing there in her bikini.

"I'm envisioning shrimp scampi, scallops wrapped in bacon, roasted zucchini, maybe some eggplant? I know they're not in season, but it is my choice...um, a light couscous on the side would be nice as well. Probably a pinot grigio? Something white. We can skip the dessert. All that sugar crap makes me cranky."

"No, we wouldn't want a cranky sore winner, would we?"

"Oh, please. I won fair and square. You were running out of steam and I could have easily passed you without the side distraction."

"We'll never know, will we?"

"No," she said quietly. "We never will."

Sticking with her *life goes on* mantra, Rayne told Claire she didn't mind riding back with Trent so Claire and Brian could ride together. It only made sense and would be more awkward if Rayne refused to ride with him.

They returned to their usual discussion of athletics, Maine, the next big adventure, and favorite foods, for most of the trip. As they neared Saco, Trent dampened the mood by bringing up the Indecent Proposal.

"I really hope I haven't hurt your feelings. That wasn't my intent—"

"Trent. Please. Don't even mention this again, okay? I'm serious. All is fine. Life goes on. I truly am sorry for putting us both, especially you, in an uncomfortable situation. It was just the emotions of the day." She waved her hand casually in the air. "We're good. I really like you. You're fun to beat." She smiled and chucked him on the shoulder.

"Cheater."

"Sore loser."

"When do you want dinner?"

"Um, Wednesday works for me. I have classes Monday and Tuesday night. Is that okay? I'll even bring the wine."

"I've got it covered. Six okay?"

"Great. See you then."

She hoped he believed her nonchalant mood as she closed the car door and waved goodbye. Unfortunately he didn't stay in the SUV but rounded the hood and helped her with her bags. "Let me," he said, grabbing her cooler and putting her over-filled beach tote on top of it.

"Oh sure, take the thing with wheels. I'll manage the rest," she teased, picking up her backpack.

"True. You kicked my ass today." He coughed, pretending to cover up his laugh. "You should take the heavy stuff."

Rayne fished for her keys, finding them on the bottom of her purse, and led the way to her apartment. Trent followed her in and dropped her things in the living room. Putting his hands in his back pockets, he rocked back and forth on his heels. "So…"

"Um, want a beer or something?" She wasn't sure if he was looking for an excuse to stay or an excuse to bail.

"I'd better not. I've got a pretty early morning tomorrow. Taking the weekend off always comes back to bite me on the butt."

I'd like to take a bite of that tush. "Yeah, I hear you. My six a.m. kickboxing class will be here any minute."

"Well, since we both have early mornings, we'd better call it a night. All the sun and water this weekend has taken its toll. I'm wiped. Thanks, uh, for the offer." His eyes widened and he blushed. "For the beer," he clarified.

She knew he wasn't talking about the Indecent Proposal. He made his point loud and clear that he didn't want her. But that was water under the bridge. *Yeah, right.* More like surging rapids ready to crest over the flood stage.

"Sure. I'll, uh, see ya on Wednesday."

"Great. Yeah. See you then." Trent's beautiful green gaze slowly traveled from her toes to her eyes and her knees went weak. There was no smile on his face, no dimple revealing his lighter side, no crinkle in his eyes emanating the laughter in his heart. Instead, those emerald jewels cut a path through her heart and right down to her girly parts. *Hot damn.*

Yes, Rayne had a habit of falling in love at first sight. Yes, Rayne had a habit of misreading signals. Yes, Rayne had a habit of wearing her heart on her sleeve and getting hurt ten times out of ten. She couldn't help herself. She wanted Trent Kipson more than she'd wanted any other man.

Chapter Nine

Trent

"Dumbass," Trent muttered as he tossed fresh ingredients into his shopping cart. This was the second stupid bet he'd lost in the past two months. However, both stupid bets involved the beautiful Rayne Wilde. The odds must be in his favor.

So what the hell did that mean? That she really wanted an affair with a career bachelor and screw the fairy tale ending she'd been dreaming about her entire life? No, to truly win would mean he and Rayne could have a friendship that would last a lifetime. A platonic one.

He placed the seafood and vegetables on the conveyor belt and smiled with his mouth, but not his eyes, at the cashier who flirted shamelessly with him.

Once home, Trent wrapped the fresh sea scallops in bacon, sprinkling brown sugar on top. After setting the oven to broil, he sliced the zucchini and seasoned it with garlic, salt, pepper, and Parmesan cheese. Garlic wasn't his first choice on a date, but as long as they were both eating it…*hell,* what was he thinking? There'd be no homeruns tonight. Not even so much as first base. Friends. A friendly dinner. Enjoyable conversation. And a beautiful woman.

Trent was doomed.

***

Rayne

"The denim mini-skirt or blue capri pants?" Dressed in a light pink bra and matching panties, Rayne held up both and checked out her reflection in the mirror. "The skirt shows off the legs, not that he hasn't seen them before. The capris enhance the butt. He's sort of seen that." She turned and eyed her butt in the mirror. "Too bad he doesn't give a rat's ass about either." Rayne sighed and plopped down on her bed. "I know I'm totally doomed when I have full-fledged conversations with myself."

She looked at herself in the mirror and sighed again. "If you got a dog or a cat or even a freakin' gerbil you could justify talking out loud and carrying on a conversation in your apartment. You wouldn't be considered a total freak." Rayne snorted, giving her reflection an eye roll. "Whatever. Capri's it is. No need for easy access. This girl ain't gettin' lucky tonight."

She turned away from the mirror and shimmied into her clothes. After buttoning up her pink sleeveless blouse, Rayne slipped on pink flip-flops decorated with a big fluffy flower and studied her reflection one more time.

"Oh, screw it." She undid two buttons and checked out her cleavage. Not Hooters material but not too shabby, either. Gathering her purse and popping a mint in her mouth, she closed her apartment door behind her and headed to her car, cursing the turmoil in her belly.

Right on time, Rayne rang Trent's doorbell. She had barely taken her finger off the button when he yanked the door open and smiled.

"Hey, I thought you'd never get here. Come in." He wrapped his hand around her wrist and pulled her in.

"Um, I didn't mix up the time, did I?"

"No, but I took the scallops out of the oven twenty minutes ago and I don't know how long they'll stay fresh. Here. Try one." He slid a scallop in her mouth before she could protest.

"Ohmigod," she said around a mouthful of deliciousness. "This is aweshome." Trent smiled and picked up another. Rayne held out her hand. "Wait." She chewed and swallowed. "Let me process. Wow. Amazing. How did you do that? I've had scallops and bacon before but…wow."

"It's the brown sugar. It caramelizes on the bacon. And you thought you didn't have a sweet tooth. Here." Trent plucked another off the plate and held it up to her mouth.

Afraid of the intimate contact, she reached out her hand, grabbing the little piece of heaven, and bit into it. The saltiness of the bacon, tenderness of the scallop, and surprisingly sweet taste on her tongue hit so many senses at once. Kind of like Trent.

No. Exactly like him.

Getting hot around the collar and she'd only taken four steps into his condo. How the heck would she survive an evening with the man of her dreams?

"Wine?"

"Mmm, what?"

"Would you like some wine? You said pinot, right?"

"Yes, please. That would be great." She followed him into the kitchen, where an array of delicious aromas filled the air. "Oh, wow, Trent. I figured you could cook, but I didn't know you could *cook.*"

"You haven't even tasted the grub yet. Save your compliments until you've tried my dessert."

"You know, this has only encouraged me to kick your butt at many more contests. I love winning. And I think cooking a meal should be my prize every time."

Trent barked out a laugh. "Pipe down, pipsqueak. First, you haven't eaten anything yet. Well, an appetizer, but that hardly counts. Second, I don't plan on losing to you ever again. And third, I don't plan on betting ever again for the rest of my life."

This time Rayne laughed. "As if. You're a gambling man if I ever met one. I give you one week before you take on another bet."

"Nice try. I'm not falling for that one." Trent tossed the shrimp in a sauté pan and swirled it around with the expertise of a gourmet chef.

After the most amazing meal she'd ever tasted,

they did the dishes together and moved out to his deck to enjoy the evening breeze.

"How about a game of chess?" Rayne tapped at the base of her wine glass.

"No."

"Uno?"

"No."

"Strip poker?" Trent eyed her suspiciously. "Kidding. Geesh, you really don't like to lose, do you?"

Trent sighed. "I'm not worried about losing, but I'm not making any more bets."

"Ha! You don't like losing to me. I never said anything about making a bet. I was just thinking of something to do." *That didn't involve taking our clothes off.*

And it was all her fault. *Stupid, stupid, stupid.* Coming up with ridiculous games to play only made her seem more desperate. They needed to stick to outdoor activities that didn't require as much conversation.

"We could hike Mt. Washington or something next week. It's your pick, but since you went to all this trouble over dinner I don't mind planning it." She avoided eye contact, not wanting to see any lingering pity in his eyes.

"Um, sure. Whatever you feel like doing is fine with me."

Her heart sank. Trent didn't sound excited. More like he was pacifying her. Avoiding conflict so as to not hurt her feelings. Yeah. She understood that tactic.

"Well, thanks for dinner. I'm going to head out.

I'll be in touch." Rayne shot up and opened the slider, letting herself in his house. She snatched up her keys from the counter and was nearly out the front door when she felt his presence behind her.

"Rayne." His deep baritone stopped her in her tracks. She kept her back to him and her hand firmly on the doorknob. "Thanks for coming over. Dinner was…nice."

What? Dinner was nice? Why the heck was he thanking her? Realization dawned on her once again, making her feel even more like a fool. A pity thank you. Something she would have said to a man she was not interested in after a date. Rayne closed her eyes and forced back her tears.

Somehow her mind sent the message to her hand to turn the knob and she let herself out of his home…and most likely, his life.

***

Trent

Two weeks went by with no word from Rayne.

Trent had never been turned down by a woman before. Damn if this didn't feel like some sort of rejection. The days rolled into each other, making each cake, each pastry, each new confection blend into the next. He'd made another quick trip across country and had been tempted to call Rayne after his final screen test. She'd appreciate his storytelling about the eccentric film groupies he'd encountered while in LA and encourage him to follow his dreams. He couldn't share this experience with her. He'd seen the hope in her eyes. Rayne might be telling herself that she could handle a quickie affair, but he knew better and wouldn't lead her on. For once, Trent's future was looking bright. If everything went according to plan, he'd be packing up his condo and moving west before Christmas.

Trent felt bad leaving his sister and Brian and his little niece behind, but they had each other and wouldn't miss him too much. He'd visit a few times a year. It was leaving the woman who made him laugh, who challenged him, who turned him on more than any other woman ever had, that made him sad.

Brian razzed him about his sullen mood, and no amount of beer, pizza, and Red Sox wins could get him out of his funk. Only one thing, one woman, knew how to test him, provoke him, and turn him on.

And he turned her down flat. What the hell was he thinking? Damn, he worried and over-analyzed more than a woman. He needed to get laid.

Unfortunately only one woman held his interest. And she was completely out of his reach.

"Dude, you in?"

Trent studied his cards. "I fold, and I'm outta here."

"Come on, Kip. It's only nine. Faith isn't even in bed yet. Stay for one more round."

The other men sitting around the poker table sighed and pushed back their chairs.

"Ah, come on, Trent. Now everyone is going to leave," Brian whined.

Jerry, the fire chief at Brian's station, stretched and slowly stood. "I gotta go too, man. Jillian's been after me about all my night shifts. Seems I should be home at a reasonable hour."

Tim snorted. "Jer just wants to get laid."

"Yeah, that too." Jerry laughed.

"Well, if you guys leave, we might as well go too." Dave shoved another handful of peanuts in his mouth before scooping up his winnings. "I kinda like Kip's girly mood. It's the only way the money falls my way."

Tim followed Dave out. The two were inseparable in every way. No one at the fire station commented on their relationship. It was the old, "Don't ask, don't tell" policy but everyone knew. And it didn't seem to bother anyone. What they did behind closed doors was their business, just like what happened behind Trent's was his. Not that anything was happening behind or in front of his doors.

"Thanks, man. Sorry for bailing out. I'm just not feeling the poker vibe tonight." Trent picked up the empty beer bottles and carried them into the kitchen.

"Dude, just call her."

"Don't know what you mean, man." Trent went back in the living room to clear the peanut mess. His friends were slobs and Claire would have his balls if he left her a mess to clean in the morning.

"Kip." Brian grabbed the empty chip bag out of his hands. "Trent. Something's gotta give. Just call Rayne and tell her you're wrong."

"I'm not." Brian laughed. "Okay, maybe I am,

but I didn't do anything this time."

"So what's the deal with you two? What happened to your Disney relationship? Kayaking trips and crap?"

"Dunno." Trent shrugged. "Guess she moved on."

"Moved on? Thought you guys were just friends? I didn't know people moved on from friends."

Exasperated, Trent rolled his eyes and pulled out his keys from his pocket. "Gotta go, man. Thanks for the beer. Next poker night is at my place."

***

Rayne

"You should just jump his bones. Take what you want."

"Sage!" Rayne glared at her sister over her wine glass.

"Wow, who would have thought our loveless sister would ever suggest such a thing?" Thyme muttered before biting in to a chip.

"Sarcasm isn't pretty or cute, Thyme. You're in no condition to offer love advice."

"Oh, stop it you two. Seriously. I thought we could have a girls' night out, not a night of bickering." Rayne filled her glass with the rest of the chardonnay and slid some more chicken nachos on to her plate.

"Our big sister is heartless—"

"Better than being too dumb to—"

"Stop it!" Rayne stood up, knocking the table and spilling her wine. "I didn't ask you two to come over to pick on my love life—"

"Or lack thereof," Sage muttered.

"Or to pick on each other," Rayne said, ignoring her sister's comment and mopping up the spill on the table. "With Mom and Dad gone for the next six months, I figured it was time for us to start acting more like sisters."

"Leave it to Pollyanna to—"

"Shut up, Sage." Rayne's outburst quieted both sisters. "I'm serious. We need to talk about Mom and Dad. And us. This," she extended her arm across the mess on the table, "isn't helping." She sighed and lowered herself to her chair. "Let's face it, Mom and Dad are crappy parents. Always have been, always will be. All we have is each other. They've taken off for God knows where and who knows when we'll see them again. Girls, we need to be close again. Like we were when we were little."

"Yeah, back when Sage wasn't a bitch," Thyme said with a smile.

"And when Thyme listened to her elders," Sage teased.

"Yes, you are my elder. I'll try to listen better to you."

"Shut up, little punk." Sage clinked her wine glass to Thyme's and then Rayne's. "To sisters," she said.

"To sisters," they echoed back.

Rayne bit back her tears, her clouded gaze moving from sister to sister. If only she had Sage's courage and confidence and Thyme's free spirit,

Rayne would be able to face Trent and actually go after what she dreamed of. *What if…what if…*

"Don't think about what if," Sage said, interrupting her thoughts. She was good like that. They'd always been closer, and acted more like a mother hen to Thyme. "Honestly, Raynie, I've seen you when you think you're head-over-heels in love. That's when you act stupid."

"Hey—"

"Shut up. You do. Don't try to tell me otherwise. You turn all Pollyanna, believing the world is perfect, along with your man of the hour. This time, no, this time is different." Sage swirled her wine, set it down, picked off a chunk of chicken from the nachos and slowly chewed. "This guy, your baker man, he's different. Totally into you, not just your body. The fact that he turned down no-strings-sex says he's just your type."

"You offered him no-strings sex? Why didn't I know about this?"

Rayne smiled apologetically at her sister. "I was going to tell you, I just happened to see Sage first." Sort of a lie. She saw Sage first because she called her first.

"Okay, I can get beyond that part, but I can't get beyond you offering free sex. Holy freaking cow. I don't even know you anymore. So I take it he said no? Wow. The man is either gay or…I don't know. What else is there?"

Feeling guilty once again for leaving Thyme out, Rayne decided it best not to fill her little sister in on how her relationship with Trent got started. Instead, she started with the most important.

"Trent and I get along really well, Thyme. He's perfect for me. We hang out, do all the adventure sports I've been dying to do since forever, he can cook like a god and obviously bakes like one too."

"You're eating sugar now?"

"No, I haven't stepped that far off the ledge. Yet. Anyway, I told him I wanted to take our relationship to the next level. You know…have sex. And he said no."

"No? Just like that? Why? Why would any red-blooded male say no to sex?" Here lay part of the problem with Thyme. She enjoyed men a little too much.

"Trent is an honorable man. He said he was afraid it would ruin our friendship."

"There's gotta be more to the story than that."

Rayne sighed. Her sisters knew her too well. "I told him about my past relationships and that I tend to…sort of fall in love at the drop of a hat. Trent is a great guy but he's not into relationships, commitment, the happily ever after that I'm into. He knows I want all of that and he can't give it to me. So…no sex for us."

"That's just wrong." Thyme finished off her wine and scraped up the last of the salsa with a tortilla chip.

"Raynie," Sage said. "You want to, don't you? You're willing to risk your heart just to get closer to him, aren't you?"

She nodded and rose from the table clearing the platter and her wine glass. Unfortunately, her head was not quite so easy to clear.

***

Trent

Closing up the bakery in the afternoon was therapeutic. He had the kitchen to himself while Marie finished the paperwork up front. The familiar scents of vanilla and sugar filled the air while his hands kept busy kneading the dough for tomorrow's bread. Images of Rayne played through his head, and his groin tightened. Trent gave up on the proper technique to make sure the dough was light and airy as his hands squeezed, imagining it was Rayne's skin. Her butt, her chest. His mind took over and soon he forgot his surroundings.

Skin as pure as silk slid under his palm as his fingers itched to find the curve of her hip, then the indent of her waist and the swell of her chest. He imagined his mouth slowly working its way from her wet lips down her silky neck to her—

"Am I interrupting?"

Trent jerked his eyes open and nearly dropped the dough on the ground. "Hey! Hi, no. I'm, uh, I'm kneading dough." Damn, she was beautiful. Rayne's hair fell in soft ribbons around her face. She didn't wear it down often and it gave her a sexy, innocent appeal. Her hair pulled back in a ponytail made her appear sexy and innocent as well. Rayne could wear a paper bag over her head and she'd still turn him on.

Long, toned legs—the same legs he'd imagined earlier—traveled miles until they reached the ragged hem of incredibly short denim shorts. Her teal tank top didn't quite meet the top of them, revealing a hint of tanned skin.

"Trent?"

Damn, busted again. He couldn't hear her over the loud *thump* of his heart. "Sorry, I'm a little distracted right now." *A lot distracted by you.*

"Think you can escape from this hell hole? Or is the boss still busting your butt around here?"

"I think he'll give me time off for good behavior." *So lame. Where the hell did that come from?* Was it his imagination or was she checking him out? He pretended to be interested in his dough ball and pounded it a few more times, but his elbow accidentally brushed up against her chest. He looked up, expecting her to jump back, but she leaned in closer.

"I was actually hoping you'd get time off for a little bad behavior," she whispered into his mouth.

God only gave him so much restraint, and God knew he was at the end of his rope. Dropping the dough, he plunged his hands into Rayne's hair and drew her towards his body. She didn't resist. Didn't even act surprised. When he started to pull back for air she pushed her chest into him and sucked his mouth into hers, not breaking their seal.

A part of his brain—a very small part—told him to back off. This was Rayne. A woman he deeply cared for and respected. A woman who was totally off limits. But the rest of him—lead primarily by his engorged anatomy—screamed, *yes!* They were two consenting adults who knew the repercussions of their actions.

Screw it. Literally and figuratively. Trent was

going for it. Nothing could stop this forward momentum except for—

"I'm heading out—oh, sorry. Excuse me. I'll leave and lock up." Marie backed away before Trent could come up with something coherent to say. Pissed that the moment was ruined, Trent dropped his hands from Rayne's backside—*how did they get there?*—and braced himself for the letdown that was sure to happen. And the cold shower he'd need.

"Are we alone now?" Rayne asked while reaching for the button on his jeans.

Trent looked down, fascinated at how quickly her long, slender fingers worked. Any words that would have formed got lost the second she pulled his boxer briefs away from his skin and slid her hand inside. He gasped and Rayne locked her lips on his once more.

Instinct kicked in and he quickly shed her of her shorts and underwear. His eyes were busy rolling back so he didn't get a peek, but he'd swear by the sensation under his hands she wore a lacy thong. Bracing his arms under her firm, round behind, he mumbled into her mouth, "Wrap your legs around me."

"I'm on the pill," she said between gasps and kisses.

Hell. So caught up in her taste he nearly forgot the one thing he swore he'd never do: have sex without a condom. There was no way in hell he'd allow a girl to show up at his doorstep making that dreaded announcement. His jeans were around his ankles and he couldn't tear himself away from

Rayne's mouth, or her ass, to grab his wallet.

"You sure?" With any other woman he'd stop and make sure they had double, hell, triple protection, but he trusted Rayne when she said she was on the pill even though he knew how much she wanted kids. Not this way. Not before marriage. She'd made it clear she wanted the happy family deal, not just a kid.

"Sex. I want sex with you. Now," she breathed into his mouth, and all coherent thoughts disappeared.

Somehow he backed them to the wall of the walk-in freezer and lost himself deep inside her. He'd never had sex without the latex barrier and damn if he could last more than a few minutes. Rayne felt too. Damn. Good.

It was over too soon and he couldn't move. Thankfully the freezer helped support Rayne, because his legs were useless right now. Her heart beat in unison with his as their breathing slowed and the shaking started to subside.

Rayne unwrapped her legs and slid down his still-rigid body. God, he wanted her again. Just five minutes and he'd be ready to go another round. She walked to the small pile of clothing on the floor, bent down, her glorious backside still red from his firm grip, and picked up her shorts and pink thong.

Nope. Five minutes was not necessary. Trent was good for round two right now. She shimmied into her scrap of lace and shorts and strolled to his private bathroom without a backward glance. How she could walk, he had no idea. Trent could barely stand. Maybe she wasn't affected by the amazing sex? He sure as hell was.

He liked seeing her tousled hair, dotted with dough and flour from his hands, and the red marks his whiskers left on her neck. Somehow his t-shirt had ripped. It must have been when Rayne attempted to pull it over his head. Vaguely Trent remembered moving her hands from the hem of his shirt to his shoulders to hold on while he hoisted her onto his throbbing erection.

They couldn't manage to take his shirt off, but his jeans were shed. One leg was inside out—he didn't remember pulling them completely off—and his boxers pooled at his feet. Stunned at the control that he obviously lost so quickly, he righted his jeans and pulled them up his legs.

Rayne opened the bathroom door as he zipped up his fly.

"Ball's in your court," she said as she walked out the door, not giving him a backward glance.

Chapter Ten

Rayne

Her hands trembled as she started her car. Holy cow! She did it! And no regrets. Not a single one. Only that it took her this long to build up the courage to jump his bones. And what big, strong bones he had. Rayne bit her lip to suppress her smile.

Not only had she never initiated sex before, she'd never done it standing up against a wall either. She'd always preferred the slow, romantic gestures. She needed her partner to coax her into lovemaking with gentle, sensual kisses and lots of foreplay before she could even think of doing the deed.

Apparently not anymore. One kiss from Trent Kipson had her ready for hot monkey sex. And she wanted more. Lots more. She only prayed that he'd pursue her and not run away. Now it was time to sit and wait. But for how long?

Apparently not long at all. Ten minutes after

turning off the shower, she heard her doorbell ring. Wrapped in a silk robe, her hair still damp on her shoulders, Rayne opened the door to the surly man of her dreams.

"The ball's in *my* court?" Trent stormed through her front door and into the living room, obviously expecting her to follow. Which she did. "What the hell is that supposed to mean? You waltz into my kitchen, shove my pants to my ankles, we have amazing sex, and then you take off without a single word other than that?"

Biting her lip, she shrugged and hid her smug smile. He thought the sex was amazing.

"That's it?"

"What am I supposed to say? I said everything I needed to weeks ago."

"Yeah, and I thought we agreed to keep things platonic."

"I guess I don't want to do that anymore." She peered up at him shyly now. The brave Rayne Wilde that seduced him in his bakery an hour ago was gone, replaced by the insecure girl she fought to change.

"Damn," he muttered and crossed the living room in two long strides. "Neither do I." He scooped her up into his arms and carried her into her bedroom, making her forget that insecure girl ever existed.

***

Rayne

The space next to her was cold and empty when she woke the following morning, and she didn't expect otherwise. They had made love three times during the night, and each time their passion grew stronger, yet sweeter. Before things turned in their friendship, he had confided in her about his love 'em and leave 'em attitude. Well, he may not have put it that way, but when he admitted he never spent the night in a woman's bed, Rayne filled in the blanks.

Their last bout was at three in the morning right before he left for work. In her book, that was a sleepover. Knowing he stayed in her bed, in her arms that long brought a smile to her face. Heck, nothing could wipe the glow from her face or the sated feeling from her body. Trent's heat and scent would stay with her forever. Rayne rolled over and buried her face in the pillow he used while resting in between their hot and heavy workouts.

Sexy man and sweet vanilla. Who knew she'd be attracted to a sweet smell. Oh, the irony. Her body ached in places she never knew could ache. Slowly she stretched and sat up, hugging her legs to her body. *Now what?* Was the ball back in her court? Should she call him? Text him? Or let him make the next move?

Ick. These games didn't interest her at all. It was so much easier to say "I love you" and spend their lives together forever. The cat and mouse game may interest people like her sisters, but it thoroughly stressed Rayne out.

Her bedside clock must be wrong. Eight o'clock? Since when had she ever slept past six? *Since your body was licked, kissed, and touched head to toe by the most gorgeous man in the universe.* Thankfully today wasn't an early day. She quickly dressed, downed a yogurt smoothie, and headed out the door to teach her nine o'clock Zumba class. She'd keep herself busy with her three Friday classes and drown herself in paperwork.

Friday night, a.k.a. *Date Night*, would not find her desperate at Trent's doorstep. She'd continue on like any other weekend. Either drinks with her sister or a soak in the tub and a good book.

After three workouts and a few hours of paperwork, her body still hummed and she didn't feel like being with anyone besides Trent. Rayne stopped by her favorite bookstore, picked out three fun, light-hearted romances, and drove home.

Halfway through her book and a set of incredibly pruned toes later, she drained the tepid bathwater, dried off and curled up in bed. So much for her handsome hero calling her to profess his undying love. Apparently he had enough sex to last him another night.

She may have had enough sex—no, not nearly enough—but she'd never have enough Trent. His scent, his arms wrapped tightly around her, the warmth of his body as he spooned hers, his laugh…no, she'd never have enough of him. And if she told him any of this he'd surely go running for the hills. Trent Kipson was as committed as a cage of rabbits.

Sweet on You

***

Trent

He knew her schedule just as she knew his. Sunday afternoons were always open. Damn, nearly every afternoon and every damn night was open. Their schedules complemented each other. Both were early birds and got to work before the crack of dawn.

Trent wondered all weekend if Rayne had plans Friday and Saturday night. Did she go out with a man? Her girlfriends? Did she tell them about him? Hell, since when did he care who a woman went out with and what the hell she said to her friends? Damn if he wasn't turning more and more into a woman.

During his high school years, he had worked in the bakery section of the local grocery store. When he first tried his hand at cake decorating Trent had worried his buddies would pick on him for being a sissy, but they stopped paying much attention to him when he had to quit playing sports so he could work longer hours to support his sister.

The jokes didn't come and Trent couldn't have cared less if they did. His hands were talented and he was proud that they helped put Claire through college. So why now, a decade later, did he start worrying if people thought he was a girl? Maybe it was being surrounded by frosting and flowers.

Hell, he needed man time. Some beer, a bar, a little Red Sox, and belching, farting, ball-scratching men.

Four phone calls later he felt like a damned depressed woman again. Brian invited Trent over to be the proverbial third wheel, or rather, fifth wheel. Bri and Claire had plans with another couple and Trent was more than welcome. No, thank you.

Tim and Dave were working, and he knew better than to call Jerry. Sunday was his sacred family time. Trent didn't have many guys he called on a regular basis. He spent his early twenties juggling night classes and odd jobs during the day and then worked on building his business. His employees were mostly female—and he had a 'no fraternizing with his employees' philosophy—and a few teens who worked before school.

Which left no time to build relationships. Not that he cared. He had Brian, and when he wasn't hanging with his brother-in-law, he was going out with a woman.

Except for the past two months. There had been no dating and very little man time with Brian. Rayne filled his down time, the role of friend and woman all in one tempting package. And damn if he didn't want her—need her—now.

He'd gone three months without sex and functioned nearly fine. But forty-eight hours without Rayne and he was climbing the walls. Was the ball still in his court? He had gone over to her place and screwed her brains out.

No, that's not what it felt like. It wasn't cheap. It was amazingly wonderful…hell, might as well sign himself up for a pedicure at the spa to help sop up the PMS oozing out of him. Sex wasn't wonderful. Sex was great or freaking awesome. He needed to

Sweet on You

get himself some right now.

Deciding the caveman act would be the only way to build his gonads back up to par, he picked up his cell and dialed Rayne.

And then hung up. No, calling still reeked of estrogen. A simple text listing his demands would be better.

Trent: My bed's getting cold. Come warm it up.

He hit *Send* before he could analyze it. Damn, he should have waited. He intended for the text to sound demanding but it sounded too poetic to him. He should have said, *Give me some sex*.

But that wasn't the type of guy he was. He'd never demanded sex from a woman before. Hell, he never had to ask. Women just offered.

Damn you, Rayne, for thinking I was gay. Just in case, he changed his sheets and took a shower. Settling into his recliner, he turned on ESPN and popped the top to his beer when his doorbell rang.

Like Pavlov's dog, he sprang out of his chair, and nearly his shorts, and pulled open his door. Like a mystical creature she stood on his front porch haloed in the streetlight, a light mist falling like shimmer on her hair.

Forget the mani/pedi; he needed to get himself a box of tampons.

It wasn't until the couch, kitchen table, and recliner in his bedroom had been christened that they finally realized they'd need food to keep up their stamina. "I'll order a pizza," Trent muttered as he nuzzled her neck. Rayne was still straddling him on his leather recliner and trying to catch her breath after her fifth orgasm. He owed it to her after how quickly the first few times went.

The woman made him feel like a teenager again, barely able to contain himself, and almost forgetting that sex was a give and take sport. Yeah, definitely a sport. The way they went at it they could enter as an Olympic event.

"Do you know how much trans fat is in a slice of pizza?"

"Don't care. We burned our share of calories in the last hour, and I have some ideas on how to burn any extra fat grams we may consume with dinner."

"Mmm," she purred. "Homemade pizza is a better alternative, preferably with cauliflower crust, but I don't have time for that. I've gotta get going." Rayne peeled her long, naked body off his and he instantly felt the cool air of separation.

Stay with me almost slipped from his tongue. What the hell? Had he used up all his testosterone on Sex Olympics or had he passed it all on to Rayne? The complete role reversal had him more confused than sugar-free frosting.

"Yeah, okay. I'll probably go into the Old Port." *Whoa, super cool man. Tell the woman you're going to hang out at a bunch of bars on a Sunday night that are more than likely filled with college kids home for the summer. Way to impress her.*

He stood and reached for his shorts, dropping a few curses that would make a sailor proud.

"You okay?"

So maybe he should have waited to drop the f-bomb when doing something other than putting on his khakis. "Yeah, just stubbed my toe on the chair." *Impressive, man.*

Rayne didn't seem affected by his drop in IQ or his naked body. Before he could zip his fly she had pulled her tank top over her breasts—sans a bra—and pulled on her skirt. *No underwear?* Why didn't he notice that earlier? Or maybe it was still by the front door. They undressed and redressed three times during her short visit. The missing underwear had to be somewhere. Smiling to himself, he imagined finding it later and holding on to it as a trophy.

"I have a super busy week at work, but I suppose I'll see you next weekend?" she asked nonchalantly as she rummaged through her purse.

"Uh, yeah. Sure. I'll be going up to Brian's camp for the Labor Day weekend. Feel like joining me?"

"Claire already invited me. I figured I'd see you there." She leaned in and kissed him on the lips, slowly sucking his bottom lip into her mouth. "See ya," she mumbled into his mouth as she released her hold.

And once again she walked out on him. Leaving the ball in his court, blue and hard.

***

Rayne

By noon, after she had taught Zumba, kickboxing, and spinning classes, Rayne thought she was dying. Literally. The sweat on her brow had nothing to do with her workout and everything to do with the virus she'd tried to kick all weekend. She had barely held it together yesterday at Trent's house. What if she got him sick as well? And then he spread the flu to all his customers at Sweet Spot? How selfish of her to think with her girly parts and not with her brain.

"Damn, girlfriend, you look like hell." Thyme tossed a clipboard on Rayne's desk and held the back of her hand against Rayne's forehead.

"Thanks, sis."

"Seriously, Raynie, go home. I've got this covered."

Rayne snorted.

"Seriously. I can do this. You're not teaching classes this afternoon and I can cover your morning ones tomorrow. I owe you big time for giving me a job. Go home and sleep. Have some soup. I'll have Sage bring some over."

Rayne groaned. "No, don't tell her I'm sick. She'll give me a lecture and read me all sorts of nasty statistics about germs and death and stuff."

"Who will take care of you?"

Leave it to Thyme to worry about something like that. She couldn't sneeze without calling Rayne and Sage and asking them to take care of her.

"I can manage. All I need is some sleep." She eyed her sister skeptically. "You sure you want my morning classes?" Thyme had been covering for her a lot lately, picking up the classes when her girls went on vacation.

"Tuesday is Zumba and Kick, right? Totally got it."

Sighing, but really needing the break, she caved.

"Okay. You remember how to lock up? Call me if you need anything."

"On it. Go." Thyme opened the door and led Rayne out.

The moment she opened the front door to her apartment, she ran for her bathroom and tossed up her breakfast. Gross. Next year she'd sign up for the flu shot.

Rayne's body felt stiff and not in the recently-been-used-by-Trent Kipson's-incredible-magic way. Her head ached, her stomach felt empty, yet her body felt like one false move and she'd be hurling internal organs into the toilet. And her ears were ringing. So. Damn. Loud.

Or maybe it was the phone. Falling asleep with her hand wrapped around her cell phone just in case the gym needed her had been a good idea a few hours ago. Or minutes or days. She had no idea how much time had passed since she last worshiped the porcelain god and got intimate with her guts. Nasty.

The phone vibrated and rang in her hand. "Wha…" she moaned.

"Rayne? Is that you?"

"Mm." She wanted to curl into Trent's voice—better yet, his arms, and feel the comfort of his hard body. It would most definitely make her aches go away.

"Am I catching you at a bad time?"

"Flu," she croaked. "Sick."

"Sweetheart, you sound like death."

"Mmm."

"Give me twenty minutes to close up shop. I'm on my way."

"'Kay." If her face didn't hurt so much she'd definitely be smiling. And were those butterflies in her stomach or signs of an upcoming date with her toilet? It didn't matter. Her prince was coming to rescue her. Rayne imagined smiling—she didn't have enough energy to do the actual deed—and living happily ever after.

And then she slept.

***

Trent

The door was locked. He could either keep pounding on the door until Rayne woke up or he could find the super and ask to be let in. Neither idea appealed to him. Trent would feel better about Rayne's security system if he *didn't* let some strange man into her locked apartment.

So now what? He could call Sage. Her business card was somewhere in his SUV. No, that would make him look like a desperate fool. If Rayne really wanted him to come over she would have left the door unlocked. Trent ran his hand over his face, scratching his stubble on his palm. Why the hell was he even here? The woman didn't ask for him to take care of her and he sure as hell didn't want to seem pushy. Or like a lovesick fool.

Trent shuddered. *Lovesick?* No. Lustsick, maybe. The woman was hot. Sexy. Funny. Smart. Gorgeous. Yeah, lust. One hundred percent pure lust. He wiped the figurative drool hanging off his chin and pulled his iPhone out of his pocket. One last try and then he was out of here. It wasn't like Rayne was in any condition to naked tango anyway. And there was no other reason for coming to her apartment. Sex. That's what their new relationship was about.

Trent's conscience laughed at him. And friendship. Hell, they were friends long before the sex started. Friends with benefits. Yeah, that's what this was, his inner devil chirped from his right shoulder. Just sex.

The angel on his left frowned, as did Trent. So he wouldn't be getting any benefits tonight, but he could still be her friend.

The phone rang four times before her soft voice answered.

"Hey, sweetheart. I'm outside your door. Can you let me in or do you want me to leave you alone? Let you rest."

"Coming," she whispered before hanging up.

Yeah, he would be too if he didn't stop reminiscing about Sunday's marathon sex.

All pornographic thoughts quickly vanished when she opened the door. Donned in an oversized Patriots jersey and nothing else, Rayne couldn't hide the fact that she had the flu. One side of her hair was smashed against her skull while the other side sported a loose ponytail ready to fall out of its elastic. The dark circles under her eyes only made her skin appear more ashen. Lips that were normally shiny and red were chapped and pale. Still, if she had been willing and able, he'd rip off her clothes in two-point-two and have his way with her. She looked sexy in a sad and pathetic way. His heart, previously overrun with lust, had just filled with something else he couldn't identify.

"Sweetheart." He stepped into her tiny galley kitchen, shut the door with his foot, and scooped her up into his arms. "You need to be in bed."

Her head lolled on his chest. "I was. But you called."

Guilt filled the remaining space in his heart. "Sorry. I'll go. I didn't know you were this bad."

She attempted to circle her arms around his neck but they fell quickly to her side. "No. Glad you're here." He felt her purr into his chest and his groin tightened.

Once in her room, he lay her down on her frilly bed and she instantly curled into the fetal position. Trent pulled the top sheet over her body, covering her tempting legs and the seductive curve of her hip. He walked over to the window and pulled the shade down.

"Can I get you anything before I go?"

"Don't leave. Please." Rayne opened her eyes, reached out, and grabbed his wrist.

Then that heart full of lust, tenderness and guilt, twisted. "Baby, you need sleep. I didn't mean to bother you."

"Hold me."

His jeans suddenly got very snug in the front. Since when did a woman, a sick woman nonetheless, asking him to cuddle turn him on?

Since Rayne got a hold of his heart.

***

Rayne

She had to be dreaming. But this time it was different. She could practically feel strong arms wrapped around her and a solid chest pressed against her back. And an impressive package snugged up against her butt. Rayne smiled. This was no dream. Trent, her knight in shining armor, came to her rescue and made the icky flu bug go away.

Well, maybe not totally away, but she felt much better cocooned in his arms. The steady cadence of his heart beating against her shoulder blade told her he was asleep. Not wanting to ruin the magical moment, she sighed and nestled in closer, soon drifting back to her dreams as well.

The room was dark when her eyes opened again. She felt the bed move, heard it creak, and rolled over to watch Trent adjust himself in his jeans. *Oh, damn flu!* Despite how she felt, she still craved him. But the cottony taste in her mouth and the smell—oh gawd! She needed a toothbrush—made her think better of it.

"Hey," she murmured.

"Rayne." He turned to face her and frowned. "I didn't mean to wake you."

"No, you didn't." She unfolded her legs and slowly brought herself to a seated position, holding her head to stop the spinning. Trent rounded the bed and sat next to her.

"Thanks," she said shyly. "For staying with me."

"How are you feeling?" He cupped her chin in his palm and inspected her face.

"Better. I could use some water. Or tea." *And you.*

"On it." He quickly left the room, leaving Rayne to her thoughts, which had nothing to do with kicking the flu bug and everything to do with falling in love.

***

Trent

Trent didn't let her talk him into staying the night. One rule he didn't break when dating a girl, no matter how sick. Not that he'd ever tended to a sick girlfriend before. He'd never spent the night with a woman and he wasn't going to start now. Even though it was three in the morning and he had to be at work in an hour, didn't mean he'd broken his hardcore rule. Brian would argue the technicality that Trent actually *did* spend the night, but Trent would argue back that spending the night meant you woke up together in the morning. Did the coffee, eggs, and toast thing.

Nope. Not this confirmed bachelor. Trent hung around—he'd never tell Brian that he spooned with Rayne all night—for a few hours and then left at three. Most normal people would call that the middle of the night. Hell, New Yorkers were just coming in from a night of partying at this time. And only midnight in California. A place he'd be in a few months.

Manhood in place, Trent whistled as he drove home. He continued arguing with his inner conscience as he stood under the water in his shower and got ready for work. Twenty minutes later he pulled into his bakery, unlocked the back door, and turned on the lights to his kitchen, picturing Rayne's lithe body molded to his against the walk-in cooler.

Sweet Spot took on a whole new meaning.

Chapter Eleven

Rayne

Three days. It never took that long to recuperate after being sick. She'd even called her doctor, who ordered her a round of antibiotics. Trent came by every night with soup and frozen yogurt—which she refused to eat—and cuddled with her throughout the night. Every morning she woke to an empty bed, but she still wore a smile on her face, and nothing else.

Their relationship moved from friends, to lovers, to caretaker. If that didn't say *love* what did? She couldn't admit her true feelings to her sisters, much less Trent, for fear that it would all come crashing down. Slow and steady. Trent feared relationships and was allergic to love. No, that little secret she would keep locked away until he was able to admit he felt the same way.

And she knew he did. He'd never tended to a girlfriend before. They'd had that discussion months ago when they were simply friends. He admitted to never recognizing any girl he dated as a "girlfriend" and he surely never cuddled all night when there was no sex involved. Heck, he had said clear as the Maine sky that he didn't cuddle. Back then she thought he played for the other side and couldn't quite picture a man as alpha as Trent spooning with Brian and thought nothing of the comment.

Smiling, Rayne came back to present day. He sure as heck spooned with her. Yup. Love. Whether Trent Kipson wanted to admit it or not, he was falling for her. Rayne slid out of bed and into the shower. The mirror didn't lie. She looked like crap. Her nose, always reliable, didn't lie either. She smelled worse.

Yet Trent stayed by her side and treated her like a precious gem.

Oh yeah. He loves me.

***

Trent

What's a respectable amount of time to wait after a woman has the flu before ripping off her clothes and having your way with her? He wanted to ask Brian but didn't. It had been eight days since Rayne went back to work and twelve days since he'd seen her naked. Well, ten days ago he saw her partially naked when she inched out of bed to use the bathroom. Her jersey rode up, revealing her hot pink panties. No thong, but he couldn't imagine wearing one of those things would be comfortable while lying in bed all day.

Trent shuddered. He didn't think wearing a string in his ass would be comfortable ever, but he sure did appreciate it when Rayne would forego comfort and wear the dental floss between her cheeks. Such fine, fine, cheeks. He sipped his beer and stared at the television, realizing two innings had gone by and he had no recollection of the Sox getting up to bat.

"Dude. You still not getting any?"

Trent stopped his beer halfway to his mouth and muttered a curse.

"I don't have the right anatomy to do that, my friend," Brian laughed. "I thought you and Rayne had something going?"

Trent never told his best friend that he'd had sex—amazing, mind-blowing sex—with Rayne. Brian just assumed it. Probably when Trent's mood turned over-the-top happy and he became too busy to hang out with Bri. And definitely when he and Rayne skipped the Labor Day weekend at the lake. He never denied, but never admitted it either. A man was due some privacy. Still, a part of him wanted to confide in his best friend.

Down, girl. The cuddling and almost-sleepovers weren't helping his masculinity any. Faith's cries snapped him out of his thoughts. "Is Faith okay?"

"I swear the girl knows when her mama is gone. She doesn't nap for longer than an hour when I'm on baby patrol but will sleep all afternoon with Claire." Brian got up and went down the hall toward the crying baby. By the time he returned, Faith was giggling and drooling.

Trent smiled at his niece and put his beer down so he could hold her. "Hey, angel." She always had this smell. Clean. Sweet. Innocent. Similar to…no, he wouldn't go there.

"Claire just texted. She'll be home from work in an hour. She has a play date with her girlfriends and their babies later. Tonight good for a poker night?"

Long overdue poker with the guys, or a game of strip poker with Rayne? Easy decision.

"Can't. Got plans." He blew raspberries on Faith's belly and handed her off to Brian. "Gotta go."

"What? You've been here for twenty minutes." Realization must have set in. "Dude," he dragged out. "You've got a date with Zumba."

"Shut it, man."

Trent tried to tone down the goofy grin as he drove home to take a shower before meeting Rayne, and was barely able to keep a straight face while he shaved, nicking himself twice in the process. They'd joked about strip poker or checkers or chess. Strip chess would be a guaranteed win for him since she'd never played before.

Tonight's agenda was a surprise. Wild monkey sex on his chaise lounge on his deck? Or on his kitchen counter? Or his workout bench? Or the stairs?

Hell, he still had rug burn from the last time.

***

Rayne

"You sure you're ready for this?"

Rayne tossed her hair over her shoulder in a flirtatious manner. "You scared, sugar?"

Trent laughed. "Bring it on."

"Care to make a wager?"

"Hell no."

Rayne bit back a smile and attempted to insult his manhood. "You're scared that a woman who has been down with the flu for a week is going to whip your butt zip lining?"

Sighing, he ran his fingers through his hair. "What's the bet?"

"Can we decide when we finish?"

"Hell no."

"You're no fun." She pouted.

Trent surprised her at work after her last class. He had a cooler all packed and followed her home so she could shower—alone, unfortunately—and dress for their hike and outdoor adventure.

"Fine. We'll keep it simple. Winner chooses dinner. When, what, and where."

"I can handle that. I'll come up with my menu while I'm waiting for you to catch up."

"Hah!"

Rayne shimmied into the harness similar to the contraption at the rock wall place and a tall, young, attractive employee fastened her straps. Trent's glare and red cheeks didn't go unnoticed. He didn't approve of another man's hands near her crotch. She held on to the man's shoulder for support. And to annoy Trent. "What's your name? Seeing how you have your hand on my butt, I figured I ought to know."

The man laughed. "Drake. And you are?"

"Rayne. Nice to meet you, Drake," she said coyly, batting her eyelashes at him and enjoying Trent's jealousy.

"I can do the rest." Trent tried muscling poor Drake out of the way.

"Sorry, sir. Policy says every person must be checked and rechecked by an employee. Insurance and all."

Rayne shrugged and smiled at Trent.

"Rayne," he growled.

After another employee checked her harness and helmet strap and hooked her up to the line, she winked over her shoulder at Trent, who was being checked over by two other Sunday River employees. "Meet you on the flipside." She blew him a kiss, held onto the rope, picked up her legs, and pushed off the edge, squealing in delight. The rush of the wind blowing through her hair as she breezed over the treetops was exhilarating. She scanned the horizon and stared below at a deep ravine and streambeds that were nestled just off the now-vacant ski trails.

Her body felt weightless, free of every burden and stress that she wore day in and day out. Her parents, keeping her sisters close, her business, her sex life. Ah, her sex life. Flying down the zip line was almost orgasmic. *Almost.* Trent could make her fly faster and higher than a 750-foot drop any day of the week.

She heard a shout from Trent and admired his

taut, hard body and enormous smile. He hollered like a little kid, obviously enjoying his run. He passed by her so she could only make out his delectable buns, but that was okay with her.

After a series of runs through the woods and the mountain, the rush began to slow as they neared the end. Trent had made touchdown and watched her finish her race.

"How was it?" He pulled her to him and kissed her quickly on the lips.

"Amazing is too simple a word. Wow. What a rush!"

"I thought you'd like it. It took you long enough to get here. I had plenty of time to come up with a menu for dinner," he teased.

They took the shuttle back to Trent's car and ate their picnic at one of the tables at the rest area.

"You up for a hike now?"

She wanted to say, *I'd go anywhere with you* but knew that would scare him away. Simple and sexy. That was their relationship.

An hour into the hike he led them off the trail and deeper into the woods. "Are you sure this is a good idea?" she asked. "You hear about hikers getting lost in the woods all the time."

"We're not going far." His voice was gruff and almost…irritated. They hadn't talked much during the hike. Rayne followed closely behind, thoroughly enjoying the view. Could he be mad at her for some reason?

"Trent. Are you okay—"

He turned around and roughly grabbed her, pulling her body into his. She felt his need, his urgency, in his tongue and through his jeans. Before she had time to process, her jeans were unzipped and shucked away. He had one hand on her butt, the other pushing away her bra for easier access to her breasts.

"Oh, God," she moaned.

"Rayne," he gasped into her mouth. "I can't wait any longer." Dropping to the ground, he pulled her on top of him and plunged deep into her body, soul, and mind.

***

"Did I hurt you?" Trent sat up a while later, after he'd given her the ride of a lifetime. Rayne was still straddling him, her legs wrapped tightly around his body.

"God, no." She leaned her forehead on his shoulder.

He was always so sweet after they made love. "I'm sorry if I—"

"Shh, don't apologize. That was…wow." Rayne lifted her head and kissed him tenderly.

"I don't know if I can hike much farther. I'm getting too old for these outdoor adventures."

"Oh?" Rayne pulled away suddenly and stood. "You do this often, do you?" She tried to tease and hide the hurt behind her eyes. Trent Kipson was a virile man. He'd obviously had lots of sexual adventures with his women and Rayne was used to vanilla bedroom sex. Another example of how wrong they were for each other.

"Can't say I do."

After zipping up, she glanced sheepishly at Trent, who had already righted himself.

"Crap. Uh, Trent?"

"What is it?"

"We sort of forgot to…well, um, we didn't use protection."

He swore and clenched his fists. The look of dread on his face hurt more than it should have. She didn't want to get pregnant right now either, but it wouldn't be the end of the world.

"You said you were on the pill, so we're safe, right?"

"Yeah."

"And I'm clean. I always use protection and have regular check-ups."

"Um, yeah. Me too." No, he didn't *always* use protection. Their first time against the freezer door of his bakery kitchen they'd forgone the condom and relied on her birth control. And she didn't need to be reminded that he was a regular in the condom-buying department.

"You're not pregnant. I mean…there's really no chance…"

"No, no chance. I haven't missed any pills. Even when I was sick. I've been on the pill for a long time and have never had any…problems." *Eat that! Yes, I've been having sex before I met you.* Not that she could remember a single sexual encounter before him. Trent sort of wiped everyone else from her memory.

"Good. Good. 'Cause you know I don't want kids. It's…I just…yeah."

"I know." She turned away from him and fixed

her bra, squeezing her eyes shut to block the tears from flowing. God, she was stupid!

The hike back to the parking lot was quiet and tense. If he hadn't made it clear before that he didn't do relationships and commitment, he sure as hell clarified it today. Being dumped by a fiancé, heck, two fiancés, didn't hurt as much as this. Looking back on her previous relationships, Rayne could honestly admit that she wasn't upset about losing her fiancés; it was about the loss of a possible marriage. She dreamed of the fairy tale so desperately she convinced herself any man would do.

She'd been fooling herself. No man would do. She wanted and needed Trent Kipson more than she needed to breathe.

***

Trent

"I've got an early start tomorrow, so I'm going to go." Trent kissed Rayne lightly on the lips and watched her open the car door.

"Yeah. Me too. Thanks for today. I had a lot of fun."

"And I believe you owe me dinner. I'll call you this week and let you know what to shop for." He winked and fled before he could say anything stupid. *Way to kill the mood, Kipson.* He'd hurt her with his words, that was obvious. Trent didn't mean to. He'd just needed to be clear about their future. Ground things a bit before their relationship got out of control.

Hell, he lost control the day she came into the bakery and had her way with him. No, he lost it before then. When she stripped down to her turquoise bikini at the lake. No, before that. When he kissed her the first time, proving he wasn't gay.

Shit. No, damn it. He lost it the second he walked into her studio and watched her shake her ass in unison with her chick music.

Now he had to figure out how to keep their relationship from worsening, from falling in any deeper. From hurting Rayne any more than he already had. Maybe it was time to end their sexual tryst and turn their relationship platonic again. But how the hell could he keep his hands off her? She drew him in with her laugh, her scent, her soft touch. No, he couldn't quit cold turkey on her. He needed some distance from her and then things would go back to normal.

He'd call the Cooking Network and let them know he'd be moving to California earlier than expected. He needed time to find an apartment and get a lay of the land anyway. Three thousand miles should be enough to extinguish the flame and bring things back to normal.

But first, they'd have one more night of unbridled passion.

***

Rayne

"What? You can't change the bet. You said no

surprises."

"The bet said the winner got to choose the when, where, and what, and the loser had to comply."

Rayne tapped her fingers on her keyboard and sighed into the phone. "So tell me the new deal." She saved the spreadsheet she was working on, closed her computer, and leaned back in her office chair.

"I'll pick up the groceries, but you have to eat what I have planned. And how I've planned it."

"Care to clarify?"

"Nope."

It sounded like the old Trent was back and she trusted him completely. Too bad it took an entire week for him to call her and cash in on the bet. He texted her on Tuesday to say he'd been busy but would be in touch. Rayne assumed it was his way to end things, so she bought stock in Doritos and gained nearly five pounds in one week.

"Fine. But I refuse to eat anything disgusting."

"Care to clarify?"

"Like snake or buffalo testicles or—"

"Ouch!" She could imagine Trent covering his crotch with his hands. "Trust me. Buffalo testicles are not on the menu. Who the hell eats those?"

"I saw it on a show this week." Oops. She revealed too much of her hand. Trent knew she didn't care for television, especially frivolous shows. But when the love of your life tells you he doesn't want you to bear his children and that he has sex with other people, well, a girl tends to go a little crazy and binge watch stupid television.

"Just trust me on this one. I guarantee you'll end

up liking what I have in store for us."

Us. Oh, that sounded good. "Okay then. When and where?"

"My place. Tonight. Six."

She glanced at the clock on her wall. That only gave her four and a half hours to primp. "I'll be there." She didn't mean for it to come out so throaty, and smirked when he cleared his throat and stammered out some gibberish before hanging up.

***

Trent

This night would either be the biggest mistake of his life or the cure for it. Hopefully, after the marathon sex that he had planned for them, he and Rayne would end their sexual relationship on mutual terms and continue their friendship. But he needed to carry out the fantasy he'd had for months, otherwise he'd always regret it.

Making sure everything was situated in his bedroom, Trent checked on the chocolate sauce that simmered on the stove and the fresh fruit in the fridge. Right on time, the doorbell rang.

He counted to ten and thought about the audit that was being done on Sweet Spot, on the lawyer jargon in his contract with the Cooking Network, and the transmission that probably needed replacing in his SUV.

Trent opened the door to a smiling goddess, and all his distracting thoughts fled and his shorts grew tight. "You look beautiful."

"Oh. Thanks."

Only Rayne Wilde could make a simple pair of khaki shorts and blue T-shirt look sexy. Maybe he could have toned it down a bit with "nice" instead. Hell, she had him in knots.

"Come in." He backed away and ushered her in, her arm casually brushing up against his as she passed by.

She walked into the kitchen and looked around. "So, what's on the menu?"

"You."

***

Rayne

There were no smells emanating from the kitchen or makings of food on the counter. One small pot sat on the stove, but other than that, everything was neat and tidy. She felt his body press up against her back when he whispered in her ear, "You."

Chills ran down her arms and to the tips of her toes. Trent wrapped his arms around her and nuzzled her neck. She closed her eyes and leaned into him, enjoying the brush of his lips on her ear. She felt the tug of her earlobe as he sucked on it and she swallowed. Hard.

"That's…great for you, but…" She tried to form a complete sentence, heck, a complete thought, but his hands, moving up to cup her breasts, made it difficult for her to form words. "What am…I going to eat?"

Trent released her breasts from his hold, rubbed his hands down to her waist, and turned her around. "Sit," he said as he lifted her onto the counter. This was definitely not what she expected, but she wasn't going to complain. He walked to his stainless steel fridge and pulled out a tray of fresh fruit. She smiled, knowing he had made the platter with her in mind.

"This is surprising. I thought you only ate fruit if it was coated in a pound of sugar or topped on some decadent dessert."

Trent raised his eyebrow and smirked. Her girly parts hummed with anticipation. He plucked a large, juicy strawberry from the plate and held it to her lips. She opened and bit into it, the juices spilling from her mouth. Rayne reached up to wipe her mouth, but he placed his hands over hers and leaned in, licking the juice from her chin.

"More," she said breathlessly.

He held the strawberry to her lips, allowing her the rest. Slowly, he leaned in and kissed her, taking some of the juicy fruit with him. "So sweet," he murmured into her mouth and pulled away before she could take the kiss any deeper.

Her mind raced with conflicting images from an angry and confused Trent to an erotic and attentive Trent. She thought their awkward moment in the woods put a kibosh to their sexual relationship—hence the Dorito-stained fingers and excess baggage on her ass—but she must have read him wrong.

Trent pulled out a stainless steel bowl from the fridge and lifted a layer of Saran wrap.

"That looks like a bowl full of sugar. You know

I don't like sweets—"

"Whipped cream. Open."

She shook her head. No way was she going to consume any more unnecessary calories this week. Besides, the mound of cream didn't excite her. But the emerald eyes sure did.

He dipped his finger through the frothy mixture. "Open," he said again.

"I—" Trent slipped his cream-coated finger in her mouth and she instinctively sucked on it. It wasn't the sweet cream that curled her toes but the salty, warm finger in her mouth that made her beg for more. She swirled her tongue and sucked. Hard.

Trent growled and pulled away, her lips smacking together when he left her.

"Damn, woman."

Rayne ran two fingers through the whipped cream and reciprocated the action, holding the white confection to his lips. He kept his gaze on her eyes and teased her palm with his tongue, working his way across her hand and down the length of her pointer finger. He licked and loved, sending tingles and butterflies to her core. She closed her eyes and tilted her head back. "Oh, Trent."

He played with her heartstrings, gently plucking one chord after the other, making a melody of music with her body. She felt the tug of his mouth all the way to her core. Rayne flexed her thighs and tried to relax, but he stirred so much desire in her.

He kept her fingers in his mouth as he scooted her closer to him and used his hands to wrap her legs around his body. Effortlessly, he picked her up, carried her to his bedroom, and set her down gently on his bed. "Don't move." He left and before she could register what was going on, he returned and set a bowl on the nightstand.

Trent lifted her shirt, exposing her belly, and reached over her body, bringing back with him a spoon full of…chocolate? He drizzled the warm liquid on her stomach, stared into her eyes, and opened his mouth to speak. Only no words came out. Instead, he lowered his head to her midsection and languidly licked the chocolate that pooled in her belly button and down her sides.

"You taste so good."

Needing to lighten the mood before she hollered out her undying love to him, she laughed. "No, I think that's your cooking."

Trent lifted his gaze to her, resting most of his weight on his elbows at her side, and slid his hard body over hers. They stared at each other, and she swore she could see his soul. Yes, he cared about her. She could sense it in the intensity in his beautiful eyes, his touch, his taste. Only he was too stubborn to see it for himself. She smiled to herself and a sense of peace that she hadn't felt since Trent came in and spun her out of control flowed through her from head to toe. Rayne's body relaxed and succumbed to Trent and all he offered.

She didn't worry about putting on a show or keeping things light and distant. Instead, her limbs loose and ready to be loved, she gave her heart over to Trent and let him have his way with her.

When he'd carried her into his room, she barely noticed the candles or the array of tiny dishes set up on a tray on the other side of the king-sized bed. He made quick work of stripping her of her top and bra and sampling the different sauces from her body.

"Mmm, my favorite is the strawberry sauce on your nipples." He undid her zipper with his teeth and rubbed his hands down her calf. Trent's mouth left a slippery trail down her stomach and nipped at her hip. Oh, the man was talented! Taking his time, he moved lower and lower until he kneeled by her feet. Picking one foot up and resting it on his shoulder, he reached over to the tray and dribbled something warm down her leg.

"Butterscotch. One of my other favorites." The next few moments were pure orgasmic bliss as he licked the trail of sticky sweetness all the way to her core. He didn't let her come up for air at all, claiming he needed to test and sample multiple combinations to find the perfect match.

And there were multiple, *multiple* combinations.

***

Trent

"My turn," she said very breathlessly after her second orgasm. Trent tilted his head in confusion and she grinned. "You're fully clothed, which is entirely unfair."

His white shirt would be stained—hell if he'd ever find the solution to get strawberry, blackberry, or chocolate out—but it was worth it. Doing his damnedest to go slow had almost cost him. Twice he came close to exploding in his pants, trying to think about taxes and building repairs as a distraction while nestled between Rayne's legs.

Once she got him naked, the show would be over. He'd give himself one minute, two tops before reaching pure ecstasy. Rayne reached for his zipper and he moaned. Or she did, he wasn't sure and it didn't matter. After all the noise she made, he was surprised she still had a voice.

Catching him distracted, she managed to flip him so he was on the bottom. *Nice view.* She straddled him, naked glory and all. Reaching across him for one of the sauces, she teased him, brushing her nipple across his cheek. He reached for her and she swatted his hand away. "Uh, uh. My turn. You didn't let me touch. Fair's fair."

"Yeah, but this is *my* menu. I don't remember being on it."

"Be nice and share." She reached for the blackberry vodka sauce and dribbled it from his chin to his...*oh*. Not quite where he wanted her mouth, but sure as hell close. Leaning over his body, careful not to come in contact with his penis or his sauce-laden chest, she licked from his abs to his chin, stopping just below his lip. He begged her to go an inch higher. She stopped, a devilish grin on her lips that he wanted to lick off, and retreated, making another lap with her tongue.

"Rayne," he growled.

He felt her body shake with laughter as she reversed her path and licked from his chest down to his navel and—"Don't stop. God, woman, don't stop." But she did. "I can't—"

"Shh. Don't be such a wimp. Maybe we can make a bet. How long do you think—"

He couldn't take anymore. He flipped her over, somehow managed to slide on a condom, and plunged into her over and over until he saw stars, and fell over the edge.

Still, he didn't dare read this sexual fantasy as a sign of love and devotion. Pure, raw sex. That's all it was.

***

Rayne

Holy mother of all that is beautiful. Rayne nearly wept as Trent held her in his arms, both their hearts still beating erratically. This was definitely not what she expected when he said he'd plan the menu. If this was what it felt like to lose a bet, she'd come in last over and over again.

Everything had changed. They were no longer great friends who enjoyed sex. They were great friends who knocked the house down with hungry, passionate lovemaking that could not be experienced by two people who didn't love and respect one another.

Still, she didn't plan on pressing her luck and scaring Trent away. She could feel him relax but knew he'd tense up if she suggested anything more emotional. Reluctantly she slipped from the warmth of his body.

"Hey, get back here." He reached for her hand but she was too quick.

"I'm a little sticky. I'm going to shower off real quick and head out."

"Need any help?"

"I'm good."

Ignoring his plea to stay, she gathered up her clothes and rushed off to his bathroom. If he surprised her in the shower she didn't think she'd be able to stay strong and leave. Thankfully—and regretfully—he left her alone.

Not wanting to linger, Rayne toweled off, quickly dressed, and pasted on a perky smile. Trent had already pulled on his shorts but his torso was still bare. Dark purple stains speckled his ripped abs where she missed some sauce. Tearing her eyes away from his sweet spot, she chimed, "Hate to eat and run, but I have back to back to back classes in the morning." She planted a chaste kiss on his lips and pulled away. "Dinner was…amazing. You can cook for me anytime." She winked and turned away before she lost her strength to leave.

Ball's in your court once again, stud muffin.

Chapter Twelve

Trent

Trent Kipson didn't crawl after any woman.
Ever.
Until now. He was willing to break the mother of all his rules and let Rayne spend the night in his bed. But she left him. She. Left. *Him.* The woman who fell hopelessly in love with dumbass after dumbass and agreed to marry any man who asked, turned down Maine's Bachelor of the Year. Well, she didn't exactly turn him down.

Stripping the stained sheets from his bed, Trent smiled at the memory of Rayne's face when he coated her with his sauces. Yeah, he had a shitload of a mess to clean up—literally and figuratively—but it was sure the hell worth it.

What he couldn't figure out was why she took off in such a hurry. Did he hurt her? Scare her? No, the pleasure on her face and the way her body shuddered and tensed before going limp could not be faked. Rayne enjoyed it every bit as much as he did. Her running off intrigued him. Maybe she *could* do no-strings sex.

***

Rayne

"No, no, no." Rayne threw the stick across her tiny bathroom and stormed into her bedroom. She pulled on running shorts and a sports bra, laced up her sneakers, and went for a grueling ten-mile run. Her legs ached, punishing her body for not properly stretching before the strenuous workout, but she pushed on, unwilling to slow down.

Things were going so well. Trent had finally fallen in love with her. Not that he'd uttered those beautiful words, but she knew. With every touch, every kiss, every laugh, she could read his love for her. For them.

This would scare him, push him away.

A baby. Rayne slowed enough to rub her flat, hard stomach and pictured what it would look like in a few months, full and round with Trent's child.

And then she pictured his reaction when she told him he was going to be a father. Remembering how mortified he was at forgetting to use a condom, and the possibility that it could result in a pregnancy—which it did—Rayne removed her hand from her belly and swiped her eyes. It had to have been her bout with the flu. Maybe she threw up too many times to make the pill effective? Or could it be the antibiotics? Too sick to care or to read the printout of warnings the pharmacist had handed out with each prescription, she'd taken the antibiotics right on schedule on an empty stomach, as indicated on the bottle. There was no blaring sign that said it would interfere with her birth control. Tears mixed with sweat as she finally rounded the final corner, her apartment building in sight.

Barely managing to pull her spent body up the stairs, she removed her key from the tiny pocket on her sports bra and let herself in her apartment. Stripping on her way to her bathroom, she took a long, cold shower. After turning off the water, she leaned down to towel off her legs and spotted the pregnancy stick.

Two pink lines. Double damn. It was too soon to mention anything to Trent, or her sisters. She'd wait a little longer, get confirmation from her doctor, then break the news.

***

The following weeks were a whirlwind of anticipation, laughter, and passionate lovemaking. Trent and Rayne spent nearly every day together taking advantage of the cool nights and slower business. Sweet Spot would conjure up another surge of business around Columbus Day to make up for the relatively slow and steady second half of September. With the college students gone and bathing suit season over, *In Motion* didn't need to offer as many classes.

Thyme had actually worked rather consistently during the past month. It was the longest Rayne could recall her sister holding down a job. Maybe being close to home and working for family would help ground Thyme and help her find whatever it was she was looking for. And her need for a job gave Rayne the freedom to spend more afternoons going on adventures with Trent and evenings wrapped up in his arms.

They continued their adventures, their bedroom gymnastics, and their fondness for food, but things were different between them. Not wanting to push Trent but hoping he'd ask her to stay, Rayne continued to crawl out of bed and go home after they'd made love at his place. However, when they worked out in her bed, Trent stayed until he had to go to the bakery.

Her blood work came back positive, the doctor confirmed over the telephone this morning. Twelve weeks pregnant. There were brief moments when she felt nauseous, and her nails had grown longer and stronger, but for the most part, she felt the same.

It was time to come clean. The fairytale had gone on long enough.

Dressed in skinny jeans that would probably not fit her in a few more weeks and a thin red sweater, Rayne finished slicing the vegetables for the salad and checked on the eggplant Parmesan in the oven, one of the few recipes she could handle.

The quick knock on the door startled her and she nearly sliced her thumb. Trent let himself in and dropped a kiss on her lips. "Hey, gorgeous." He stole a cucumber from the salad bowl and popped it in his mouth. "Smells great. What's on the menu?"

"You?" she teased. The familiar smoldering

shadows in his green eyes told her he wasn't opposed to the idea. After three months they still hadn't tamed their sexual desire for one another. He bent and took her mouth when his stomach growled. "Dinner first. You can be dessert. I much prefer you to…well, I much prefer you."

He didn't balk at her admission, which was encouraging.

"Mmm. I can settle for that."

Their conversation flowed, much like it always did, and Trent helped wash the dishes before he picked her up and carried her off to the bedroom. She didn't want hot and steamy sex tonight; she craved slow, passionate love. And that's what he gave her.

***

Trent

Rayne's hair tickled his nose. He brushed the strands to the side and trailed his hand down her naked spine. He rather enjoyed the feel of her warm body draped over his, her head resting comfortably on his chest. The sweat had finally dried from their slick bodies and the temperature cooled in the room. He drew the covers over them and cradled her closer, lost in the comfortable feeling of her breasts against his side.

She swirled her finger around his nipple and stopped. "Trent?"

"Hmm?"

"You're a good guy."

He laughed. "Glad you think so."

"No, really." She sat up, pulling her knees into her body as she toyed with the sheet. "I like you. A lot."

They talked about everything under the sun but never about their feelings toward one another. He hoped she didn't profess her undying love. He couldn't return the statement. It wasn't something Trent Kipson was capable of. The eggplant they had for dinner felt heavy in his gut.

"Rayne, you're pretty awesome yourself." He brushed his knuckles across her cheek and down toward her breasts. "And sexy." Trying to lighten the moment, he wiggled his eyebrows. "Want me to show you how much?"

Only she didn't let out the expected squeal. Instead her eyes turned sad and serious, a frown tugging at her lips. Was he wrong about her feelings? Maybe she wasn't about to profess her love but was going to kick him out of her bed. And her life.

Neither of the options pleased him.

"I...uh. We need to talk."

Those four words never preceded anything good. "Rayne, sweetheart. Things are good. I'm happy. You seem pretty happy. Well, you were ten minutes ago," he teased once again.

"I'm pregnant."

His hand paused mid-air before he could brush back the curl that stuck to her cheek. The air in the room closed in around him and stilled. Someone's hand—his, hers, the devil's?—clutched at his throat and squeezed. He couldn't breathe. Couldn't blink.

Couldn't move.

Rayne tilted her head up and studied him. Those chocolate eyes expressionless and empty, looking just as his father's had for so many years after Sonya Meadows left him. The years of misery flashed before his eyes—his father's depression, the drinking, the mental abuse and physical neglect. Obsession tore Michael Kipson apart, killing him and ruining his kids.

Trent would not do the same. He wouldn't fall in love and sure couldn't be a father.

"Shit. No. Impossible."

Trent jumped out of bed, jerked his jeans up his legs, and searched frantically for his shirt. To hell with his socks. "I knew this would happen," he said as he tugged on his tee. "I never should have slept with you. You wanted this all along, didn't you? A baby. A husband. The kid probably isn't even mine. We used protection. Except for…you trapped me, didn't you? You said you were on the pill. I told you I wouldn't…shit. I can't do this."

Unable to form any more complete thoughts, he stormed out before he said anything else, grabbed his keys from the kitchen counter, and slammed the door behind him.

The knife twisting in his gut nearly brought tears to his eyes as he drove home. Or was it a knife in his back? His body hurt so bad he couldn't tell. This wasn't supposed to happen. Rayne was a good, honest person. He'd never expected her to deceive him for so long. Damn him for believing their friendship was genuine. Damn him for being a fool in believing you could be friends with a hot woman without her expecting something more. She knew, she *knew,* he didn't want kids. For the first time in his life Trent opened up to a woman and she betrayed him.

Sonya Kipson taught him how to be loveless and carefree, while Michael showed him how loving someone too much would be the death of you. The hell with the Kipson curse. Trent needed to get away from everyone, even his sister, before he poisoned them as well.

And he needed to get away from Rayne and her manipulative chocolate eyes that had lured him into believing the impossible. Trent banged his head against the steering wheel when he stopped at the traffic light.

Lies. All lies. Not only Rayne's but his as well. He knew she didn't lure him into anything; it was Trent's weakness for a beautiful woman that made him believe he could have his cake and eat it too.

Trent was a Kipson. Always would be. He had too much of both his parents' blood in him, Sonya's need for freedom and Michael's vulnerability to a woman. For the past ten years Trent showed no sign of loving a woman. It wasn't until Rayne came along that he felt himself weakening like his father.

And a baby? No, he couldn't raise a kid. Kids were influenced by their parents and he had nothing to offer other than cynicism, bad blood, and a binder of cake recipes. What the hell did he know about being a father? Nothing.

Escape. He needed to rid himself of his parents and their curse before he ended up weak and helpless.

No. The baby wasn't his. He refused to believe it. Rayne wasn't pregnant. He couldn't think about her or her infectious laugh, the way her eyes lit up when she won a bet or darkened when he touched her, or her belly rounded with his child or he'd turn into a weak, whipped, nothing of a man just like his father. Deny and escape.

On his frantic drive home he called Felicia and told her he'd be in LA the following day.

***

Rayne

Thankfully Thyme covered Rayne's classes the following days. Rayne's tear ducts had dried up but her eyes were still red and swollen and the slightest song or noise, even the movement of leaves outside her window, brought her to hyperventilating tears again. Dry sobs now, the dry heaving of weepiness.

Her heart was empty and heavy, her body unable to cooperate and move. There was no way she could stand in front of a group of women with a smile on her face and encourage them to sway their hips, kick their legs, and shake their ass to the music when all she wanted to do was curl up and die. It took her nearly a week to gain the energy to go back to work, and even longer to stop crying herself to sleep.

It shouldn't have been such a shock to her. Trent made it clear from day one that he had no desire—completely abhorred the idea—of ever getting married or having kids. At the time she thought it was sad, then she grew to understand why he had such harsh feelings toward family, but her upbringing wasn't much better. Her parents were too obsessed with each other, their own children an imposition in their lives.

Only Rayne could see the fault in her parents' relationship and learn from their mistakes. That was why she was so anxious to be a mother, to love and care for a child in a way that she never experienced. Trent's accusation that the baby wasn't his hurt more than his rejection of her. If he didn't want to confine himself to marriage, so be it. He was an amazing uncle to Faith and she knew he would be a devoted father. If only Trent would believe in himself.

After a month of silence Rayne accepted the fact that she'd be raising the child on her own. Slowly she gained the courage to get up in the morning—her baby needed nutrients—and exercise—she needed to stay healthy. She would not allow her child to feel the rejection that she felt for the last twenty-seven years. Better to never know your father than to feel his animosity toward you.

Rayne would make sure her child never went a moment without feeling cared for and appreciated. She dressed for her doctor's appointment and sent her sisters a text reminder. Their supporting, loving embraces greeted her in the waiting room an hour later.

"Nervous?"

"A little." Rayne patted her slightly rounded belly. After she checked in, they found three chairs next to each other and thumbed through magazines, distracting Rayne with idle gossip from Hollywood.

"They say Jennifer Aniston is pregnant."

"She's been pregnant for the past ten years. Leave the woman alone. Not everyone wants to have kids, Thyme."

"Just because you're selfish and don't want to share your life with anyone doesn't mean—"

"Enough." Rayne adored her sisters but their opposing views on…everything…drove her nuts.

"I still can't believe you're four months pregnant. My belly is bigger than yours." Thyme crossed her arms over her stomach. She'd always been self-conscious of her curves.

"Oh, stop. You're just looking for attention," Sage scoffed.

"You're just jealous because I have bigger boobs than you."

"You have bigger boobs than everyone."

"Girls. Seriously." Rayne tossed the magazine she hadn't been reading on the table and glanced around the waiting room. Women in various stages of their pregnancies waited for their appointments. The woman across from her, looking ready to burst, leaned her head on her husband's shoulder as he rubbed her belly. Rayne imagined Trent by her side, not that she wasn't grateful for her sisters' support, whispering words of encouragement in her ear. Where would he be while she was in labor, bringing their child into the world? Out with another woman? In bed with another woman?

Rayne cringed.

"Hey, you okay? You said this was a quick check-up. We get to see how much you weigh, hear the heartbeat, and we're out of here, right?" Sage asked as she scrolled through her emails on her iPad.

"Yeah. I'm fine. Just excited. When I heard her heartbeat last month it made it so…real."

"Her, huh?" Thyme asked.

"Him. Definitely a boy," Sage confirmed.

"I thought boy last week, but when I felt her move yesterday it seemed so sweet. Must be a girl." Rayne sighed and imagined a little girl with arresting green eyes like her father.

"Rayne?" a nurse called out.

"Oh! That's you!" Thyme jumped up.

"Easy, Tiger. It's not like she won a prize," Sage said.

Rayne wanted to correct her. This little baby was the biggest prize of her life.

"Hi, Rayne. I'm Jo. I'm just filling in for a bit. Dr. Hallowell's nurse was in a car accident last week and she was already short-handed, so a few nurses from Dr. Carey's office are filling in. I'm actually heading out, but another nurse will take care of you once I take your vitals."

Nurse Jo led the three sisters into a small room, checked Rayne's blood pressure, and pricked her finger to check her iron. "Looks good. Sit tight. I'll get the nurse who will go over your prenatal care with you." Nurse Jo left the cramped space.

Sage picked up a small model of a pregnant woman. "Wow. Look at her bladder."

"I'm already making a dozen trips to the bathroom. Can't wait to be in there every ten minutes."

"Sorry to keep you waiting. I—Rayne?"

"Claire?" Rayne jumped up. "Hi."

"You are…you're pregnant?"

"Isn't that why most women come here?" Sage drawled.

"Actually, no. This is a women's clinic, so patients are often pregnant, but they also do annual exams, mammograms—"

"Okay, we don't need the lecture."

"Sage!" Embarrassed by her sarcasm, Rayne tried to alleviate the tension. "She's just nervous being in such tight quarters."

"That's okay. I, uh, I didn't know."

"Wait a minute. So you girls know each other?" Sage asked.

"Yes. This is Claire. Claire Smart. She's…"

"Trent's sister," Thyme whispered from the corner.

"And the rat bastard didn't tell you he got my sister pregnant?"

"Sage!"

"That's okay, Rayne. She's right. He is a rat bastard for not telling me and for not being here for you. No offense. I take it you're Rayne's sisters?"

"The rude one is my older sister Sage. And this is Thyme."

"I've heard a lot about you," Claire said, trying to bring some semblance of normal back to the room.

"Apparently you haven't heard much about Rayne," Sage mumbled.

"Girls, can you give me a few minutes alone with your sister, please?"

They referred to Rayne, who nodded.

"Okay. We'll be right outside. Don't be long. I want to hear my nephew's heartbeat."

When Sage and Thyme left, Claire closed the door and wrapped Rayne in a warm hug. "I am so sorry for my brother. I don't know what happened. All I know is he took off suddenly for California and told Brian and me we could look for him on the Cooking Network. He hasn't returned any of Brian's calls or texts. Brian figured you two had a fight, but he made me promise not to meddle. I tried calling a few times…"

Rayne slid from their embrace and wrapped her arms around her body. "I'm sorry I never returned your calls. I just needed to…distance myself. It hurt too much to talk to you since you're…"

"I understand, Rayne. I don't take it personally and I won't push you for details, but if you ever need to talk, need a friend, call me. Forget I'm Trent's sister, okay? Besides—" she rubbed Rayne's belly "—that's my little niece or nephew you've got in there. Faith will want to play with her cousin."

"No, I don't think that's a good idea. Trent made it very clear that he doesn't want this baby. I won't let my child feel his hatred—"

"Whatever Trent said, he doesn't hate this baby. You've seen how he is around Faith. He'll make an excellent father."

"He doesn't want to be a father."

"He may not, but he is. Okay, enough of that. Let's finish you up and get you in to Dr. Hallowell. I want to hear this little heartbeat as well."

Chapter Thirteen

Trent

Knowing his sister wouldn't pester him *this* much unless something was wrong, Trent answered his phone. "This is the tenth time you called today. Is Faith okay?"

"You got Rayne pregnant and completely abandoned her?" Claire yelled through the phone. So much for keeping that one a secret. He already felt like an ass; he didn't need anyone else to confirm it.

"Leave it alone, sis."

"I will not!"

"Yes, you will." He yanked open the fridge and pulled out two bottles of beer. Rummaging through the junk drawer, he finally found the bottle opener, ripped open one of bottles, and chugged until it was gone. Letting out a loud belch, he uncapped the second bottle and walked into his living room.

"The caveman act won't scare me away. I've seen and heard far worse."

Yeah, from their father. History repeating itself. First Michael Kipson drowns his sorrows in a bottle of beer, and now his son.

"You're pathetic."

"So leave me alone."

"No. Why didn't you tell me Rayne was pregnant?"

Trent shrugged. "It's none of your business."

"That baby is Faith's cousin. My nephew or niece."

"Who said I was the father?"

That shut her up for a good minute. "No, I don't believe that for a second."

"Really? 'Cause your silence spoke a lot."

"My silence says I don't believe it. Rayne loved you. Loves you. I can see it in her eyes."

"You talked to her?" Careful not to seem too eager, he crossed his foot onto his knee and reclined in his La-Z-Boy.

"Yes. And the baby is yours."

He knew that. He never doubted it but couldn't control the garbage that came out of his mouth that night or the lies running through his head for the following days. Weeks. Trent figured Rayne would have called, tried to convince him of that love and marriage crap. But she didn't.

"I'm helping out at Southern Maine Women's Clinic in South Portland. I've been on a waiting list to move over to that facility. There was a temporary opening. It means steady hours for the next few months, which is perfect timing with the holidays coming up. I won't have to work on Thanksgiving or Christmas. And speaking of holidays—"

"No."

"I haven't even said anything yet."

"Doesn't matter anyway. I'm not coming home."

"Oh, for crying out loud. You're coming to our house for Thanksgiving next week."

"I'm busy."

"Faith will miss you. It's her first Thanksgiving."

"Faith doesn't care what day it is and neither do I."

"You know what, I don't blame her. I don't want my child to be forced to spend time with someone who doesn't love her either. It's no wonder why Rayne doesn't want you near her child."

It wasn't until his sister hung up on him that Trent finally let out the breath he'd been holding. *Rayne doesn't want you near her child.* So she did think of him as some monster, just like Michael Kipson. Damn history. Damn genes.

Claire was right. Faith shouldn't be exposed to an ass of an uncle and neither should Trent's child. He had two options. Stay away from the people he cared about or change his freakin' attitude.

***

Rayne

For the past five years Thanksgivings were spent at Rayne's apartment. As soon as Thyme turned eighteen, Suzie and Neil Wilde began traveling during the cold New England months, leaving their daughters to fend for themselves. Rayne didn't mind. She liked the intimate dinner feast she and her sisters collaborated to prepare.

There had been other dinner guests too. Sage never brought boyfriends, but Thyme usually did—no one serious, but whomever she was dating at the time. Ironically, Rayne never had a boyfriend come to Thanksgiving dinner. Her brief engagements were in the spring and over before the end of the summer. Typical summer romance. That was Rayne.

This year it would only be the three of them, but next year they'd have a little one at the table. Rayne thought of adorable Faith enjoying her first Thanksgiving. Claire invited her to Brian's family's house but she respectfully declined, even after hearing Trent wouldn't be there.

Faith and the Wilde child in Rayne's belly would be a little more than a year apart. Already Claire was planning play dates. Rayne accepted recent invites to lunch with Claire and Faith and discovered how much she missed the two. Learning Trent had moved across the country without a simple goodbye hurt as much as him denouncing his parentage of the child.

When the Thanksgiving dinner had been eaten, Sage and Thyme told Rayne to sit and put her feet up while they did the dishes. Rayne smiled as she listened to her sisters argue in the kitchen. Placing a hand on her belly, she felt her wild one kick and shuffle around. She'd definitely make a great Zumba dancer, Rayne thought with a laugh.

Peace and serenity. She'd finally gotten there. She didn't need a man in her life to make her happy or complete and neither did her baby. Rayne had enough love in her to make up for an absent father and two negligent grandparents. Her child would never go without and never, ever feel the emptiness that Trent, Rayne, and her sisters felt growing up.

***

Trent

Trent pulled out his cell phone and texted his sister.

Trent: In parking lot Where r u

He drummed his fingers on his steering wheel while he waited for his sister to leave for her lunch break.

Claire: Running late. Come inside. I'll meet you in the second floor waiting room.

It was just like his sister to spell, capitalize, and punctuate her texts correctly. Shutting off his engine, he got out of his rental and made his way into the medical building. Not bothering to read the signs to the different offices, he took the stairs two at a time to the second floor. It smelled faintly of flowers, which was better than the stale, sterile scent of the hospital where she usually worked, and was decorated with light pink walls, plants, and feminine prints. He smiled at the receptionist.

"I'm looking for my sister, Claire Smart."

"Yes, she said to have a seat in the waiting area." The receptionist pointed toward an open space. Trent thanked her and started heading toward an empty chair when he heard a familiar voice.

"Well, that sucks."

"Sage," Rayne reprimanded.

"I'm sorry, Miss Wilde. Only one guest is allowed in during the exam," a nurse said, looking from Sage to Thyme.

Trent's breath caught in his throat. He could pick Rayne's butt out of any line-up. Her jeans molded to her rounded globes. She turned to talk to Sage and his head spun. Her long-sleeved shirt clung to her body, accentuating her curves. Her breasts were larger, as was her belly. Just a slight bump to it, nothing like the flat, smooth stomach that he licked chocolate sauce off a few months ago. His groin swelled and his jeans grew tight. He knew her body better than his own. Knew being the operative word. Not anymore.

"I'm sorry. I didn't realize I could only bring one person in with me. Can you give me a minute?"

The nurse nodded. "Sure. Let me process some paperwork. I'll be right back."

"I'm the oldest. I should go."

"No fair. I'll probably be the next one to have a baby, so I should go."

"Thyme? Is there something you need to tell us?" Rayne asked.

"No. I'm not pregnant, but we know Sage never will be."

"Easy, brat. I could—"

His brain shut down and his legs took over. Trent

walked over to the trio and said, "I'm going." The girls stopped squabbling.

"Well, I'll be dammed. Look who's risen from the dead." Sage put a protective arm around her sister.

Rayne crossed her arms under her breasts, which only accentuated their fullness. He lifted his gaze back to the pools of chocolate.

"You weren't invited to this party, bud," the sassy sister said.

"Miss Wilde. I'm ready for you. I can't wait any longer or it will cut into the next patient's slot."

"He should go," Thyme said. God bless the youngest sister.

"I don't think she wants him to go," Sage bickered.

"He's the father."

"That's not what he said."

Great, so Rayne told them everything.

Rayne stayed conspicuously quiet while her sisters argued around her, her eyes changing from round and shocked to small and distant.

"Miss Wilde?" the nurse prompted again.

Despair filled her face, her eyes and mouth turning downward in defeat. "He can come," she whispered and turned to follow the nurse.

Instead of feeling like the victor, he felt like a fool. She didn't want him in there. He didn't need to be there. Hell, he didn't even know where *there* was, but he followed Rayne down the hall, ignoring her sister's warning, "Don't you dare hurt her."

Once in the dimly lit room, the nurse asked Rayne to hop on the table and pull her pants down under her belly. She sheepishly peered over at Trent and then turned her head, ignoring him once again. The nurse squirted some gook all over her belly and glided an instrument around.

"First, I need to take some measurements, check out the heart and lungs, and then we can play around." The room was quiet as she pressed some keys on the keyboard attached to the wand and pointed out various body parts on the screen. "See the four chambers? That's the heart. Nice and strong and steady."

Trent didn't know where to look. At Rayne's smooth, slightly rounded belly, completely unfamiliar to him, or at the screen where the nurse pointed. At first the blob on the black and white screen didn't look like anything, but as his eyes became familiar with the tiny object, he started to make out the head and arms and legs. And a foot. Trent smiled. And a hand. Five tiny fingers stretched. He did that. He and Rayne made that little ball of bones and fingers that would soon be a baby.

"Oh." Rayne flinched.

"Are you hurt?" Trent jumped to her side and the nurse laughed.

"Saw that. This baby's an active one. Just gave you a one-two punch."

"Yeah. I call it my Wilde child."

Trent almost laughed but stopped himself.

"Would you like to know the baby's sex?"

"No."

"Yes."

Rayne turned and glared at him. "No."

He stared at her, soaking in her radiant skin.

God, he missed her. Missed her hair that always made its way to his pillow, causing him to sneeze. Missed her laugh; the way she challenged him and kept him on his toes. But that wasn't the woman who lay before him. She was gone, replaced by this serious, pregnant woman. He hurt her. He was the one who changed her.

"Okay. Whatever you say. We'll wait until the baby is born."

Rayne didn't comment on his use of "we." It was out before he could think of the consequences. This meant he was sticking around. He was going to be a father.

***

Rayne

Seeing Trent in the waiting room knocked the wind right out of her already squished diaphragm. She couldn't form a cohesive thought. Part of her itched to jump into his arms but most of her was wary of him. How did he know she had an ultrasound scheduled?

Claire. Rayne would see her after the ultrasound and give her a piece of her mind. How dare she betray Rayne like this?

Or did she do Rayne a favor? It was hard to tell if the flutter in her belly was the baby or her anxiety at seeing Trent after two months. Rayne figured he'd be tanned, the California sun bringing out blond highlights in his hair. Instead he looked like he'd lost some weight, the scruff on his face making him appear worn out instead of tough. She couldn't look at his emerald eyes without remembering their frantic lovemaking in the woods. So consumed in each other that they forgot to use protection. His accusation still stung and she'd never forgive him for the way he treated her, thinking she trapped him into getting her pregnant.

Oh, the nerve. The moment of weakness passed quickly, hurt and anger consuming her once again.

The nurse wiped the gel from her belly. "Okay, Miss Wilde. I'm done on this end. You can have a seat in the waiting room and a nurse will be with you shortly. You can keep these." She handed Rayne four pictures of her baby. The first was a headshot, the second showed most of the head and torso, the third was an adorable little foot, and the fourth was a hand, as if waving to its mama.

"Thank you. I'll cherish them forever." Rayne studied each picture over and over as she walked back to the waiting room.

"You have pictures! Let me see." Thyme leaned in and admired her little niece. Or nephew.

"You okay?" Sage asked Rayne, but her sharp glare was fixated on Trent.

"Yes. It was amazing. The baby moved around a lot so the nurse had a hard time getting some shots. It was…wow. There's a little baby inside me."

Sage laughed. "You're just now figuring this out?"

"I had no idea it would be so…amazing."

"So you say. Thyme, let me see the pictures of my niece."

"Can I keep one?" Thyme reluctantly handed the

pictures to Sage.

Rayne was grateful that her sisters were happy for her, but she couldn't part with any of the pictures.

"Rayne? I can see you now." Claire smiled apologetically at Rayne, her gaze shooting to Trent and Rayne's sisters before settling on Rayne again. "You're not all coming with her."

"I need to get back to work anyway. Call me later." Sage kissed her cheek and handed back the pictures.

"I'll go make sure everything is okay at In Motion."

"Thanks, guys. Really. I'll call you both later." She hugged Thyme and followed Claire, not looking back at Trent, although she sensed him behind her.

Claire, Trent, and Rayne walked in awkward silence down the hall to the exam room.

"How was your lunch?" Trent crossed his arms and leaned against the doorjamb before entering the room.

"Um, I worked through lunch. Sorry for cancelling on you."

Trent pulled out his cell phone. "Funny. No text about you cancelling."

"Funny. No text from you telling me you were moving to California."

"Can you two bicker about your lunch later? I'd like to finish my exam and get out of here."

"Rayne, I'm sorry. I—" Claire started.

"No. Don't say anything." She tried to smile, but her mouth wouldn't relax with Trent in the room.

"Okay. Here's your gown. Dr. Hallowell will be right in. Trent, you can leave now."

"No. I'm staying."

"She's had enough, Trent."

"It's my baby too. I should be a part of this."

"Even if I *trapped* you into it?" At least he had the decency to cringe.

"I don't think you trapped me."

"Really? Maybe I stopped taking my birth control pills hoping that in the throes of passion you'd forget to use a condom while I was ovulating and then you'd be stuck with me and my baby forever." She'd never heard herself speak so nasty to anyone before. And it felt good. No more Miss Pollyanna seeing the glass as half-full. Trent hurt her and she wouldn't let him off that easy.

"Trent. You didn't," Claire scolded. "The doctor believes the antibiotics she took when she had the flu made her pill ineffective and—"

"Claire, don't. He doesn't care and neither do I." She turned to Trent. "I'm not asking you for anything. I don't need child support. I don't need your pity and I don't need you around my baby making her feel unwanted."

"I won't be like—"

"Bullshit." Rayne hardly ever swore, but that felt good too. "You've made it clear from the first day I met you that you don't want kids. Nothing has changed."

"I feel guilty about—"

"I don't want your guilt and neither does my child. Now, please leave. I need to change." She turned her back to him and Claire, hoping they'd leave soon before she lost her composure.

The doctor took longer than usual, which was a blessing. Rayne had time to dry her tears and calm her shaking. The exam was quick and painless. She checked out at the front desk and bundled up in her winter coat as she walked to her car. With her head down to avoid the cold, harsh wind on her face, she didn't see Trent until she was a few feet from her car.

"What are you doing?"

"I'm starving. I figured you haven't had lunch either. Let's go grab something to eat."

"No thanks." She unlocked her car, but Trent put his hand out so she couldn't open the door.

"Rayne," he said softly. "Please. Just lunch. At a restaurant. I need to talk to you."

Two months ago she would have fallen at his feet. Two months was a long time to build walls. Hers were pretty thick.

"Please."

In all the months she'd known him he'd never begged. God, he looked helpless. And handsome.

"Fine. I'll meet you at the Bistro." She shoved his hand aside and slid into her car. Checking her rear-view mirror, she saw him jog over to a vehicle. By the time she got to the first light he had caught up with her. The restaurant was only ten minutes away and that was not nearly enough time to conjure up an escape plan. Somehow he managed to be at her car when she parked and opened the door for her before she could unbuckle.

"I'm not an invalid. I can get out of the car myself," she growled.

"Sorry."

She didn't mind his chivalrous behavior but didn't think she could keep him at bay if he kept touching her. He held the door for her and asked the hostess for a quiet table in a corner.

The waitress wrote down their order and they sat in silence, sipping their water, taking in the scenery. The restaurant was festive, not overdone in holiday decorations but tastefully decorated with poinsettias and greenery draped on the windows.

When her spinach salad arrived she was grateful for the distraction. Trent begged for her to go to lunch so he could talk but he hadn't said a word yet. He fidgeted with his napkin, his utensils, his water, looking everywhere except at her. She thought about giving him a hard time about it but then she'd have to listen to him, or answer his questions, something she wasn't ready to do.

***

Trent

After they wasted enough time in awkward silence he pushed his chowder bowl aside, resting his elbows on the table. "So."

She lifted her eyes to his and finished chewing. "So."

"We're having a baby."

"*I'm* having a baby. I told you that a few months ago."

Her hormones were obviously affecting her personality. Trent wasn't expecting the hostility.

The Rayne he knew was a peacemaker, willing to listen to all sides of the story, never quick to judge. The Rayne who sat before him was…glowing. He smiled, remembering the expression on her face when he'd beat her at chess.

"Remember when you lost our chess game?"

She lost that bet and had to dance around naked. One song, that was all he had asked. She sulked and tried to get out of her end of the bargain but he held her to it. She didn't make it thirty seconds into the song before he'd tackled her to the floor and made love to her.

"What? You're thinking about that *now?*"

"Yeah, I am," he said with a laugh, enjoying watching the blush creep up her neck and fill her cheeks.

"Well, I'm not. I'm thinking about how you threw me to the ground in the woods and didn't strap a condom on and then accused me of trapping you before moving three thousand miles away." She dropped her fork noisily to her plate and pushed her chair back.

"Don't go. Please. You're right. I was an ass."

"Not was. Are. You *are* an ass."

Trent nodded. "I deserve that. I'm sorry. I won't turn my back on you or the baby."

"You already did."

"I won't do it again."

"Why?"

"What do you mean?"

"Why the sudden change? Did Claire guilt you into it? Because that's not any better. My baby will not grow up feeling like a nuisance, someone who got in the way of her father's freedom. I'd rather her not know you at all."

Trent ran his hand across his scalp. He needed a haircut. Normally he kept it so short he couldn't run his fingers through it. Easier that way with the bakery, but Felicia said women liked longer hair these days and the hair stylist on the show would gel it up for him. When did he start letting other people tell him what to do? When he stopped hanging out with his friends, when he stopped caring, when he cared more about his career than his family.

When he stopped seeing Rayne.

"The baby isn't a nuisance."

Rayne snorted. "Not yet, because it isn't you she's kicking all night. It isn't your bladder that's as flat as a pancake. It's not your varicose veins that are going to burst. And it won't be you up in the middle of the night when she has colic and can't sleep. It won't be you when she's teething and cries for hours on end or when she—"

"Rayne. Stop. I know what you're trying to do."

"Really? What the hell am I trying to do?"

Now she even sounded like him. Could be a good thing. He knew how to handle wiseass better than crying female. "You're trying to scare me away, but it won't work. I'm going to take responsibility for the baby."

"From California? You'll squeeze her in between paparazzi and being a world famous sexy baker guy? Doubt it. You made your choice. I'm happy for you that you've gotten what you always dreamed of."

So she still thought he was sexy. He could work with that. "I will take responsibility."

Rayne stood and shoved her arms in her coat. "See, that's the problem right there." She picked up her purse and reached for her wallet.

"No. Lunch is on me." They both paused and he remembered how many times they had lunch, dinner, dessert, on each other. Never breakfast. That would scream *commitment!*

"Whatever." She stormed off before he could flag down the waitress to pay for their meal.

Before she could explain exactly what the problem was.

Chapter Fourteen

Rayne

"Let me explain," Claire said when she answered the phone.

"This better be good." Rayne filled up her tub, poured in a generous amount of lavender bubble bath, and settled herself in the frothy suds.

"Trent called last night right before he boarded a red eye flight. I asked him to meet me for lunch…but things got busy. I went to the waiting room to tell him and saw your sisters. They filled me in on the rest."

"Uh huh. And you just so happened to plan your lunch for the same time you knew I'd be having my ultrasound?"

"Okay. Guilty on that. I wasn't expecting him to go in with you. I just wanted you two to accidentally bump into each other. Seriously. The rest was…fate. He came home to see you."

"Fate has nothing to do with this."

"I know. I'm meddling. Brian told me to stay out

of it, but Trent won't talk to him either. I hope you two can work things out. I care about you both so much and know that you can compromise."

"So you think I'm at fault?"

Claire was silent for a moment. "No. Trent screwed things up. I just wish you'd give him a second chance."

"Claire, he never even tried for a second chance. Not until you thrust him in my face. Now he's feeling guilty. I don't want his guilt. I want his…" *love.*

"Rayne. You see how wonderful he is with Faith. Imagine how loving he'll be to his own child."

"Sure. For ten minutes while he's pushing her on the swing in the park. The rest of the time he'll be too busy with…his job, friends, girlfriends, his life in California."

"Trent has never had a girlfriend. Sure, he's dated lots of women, but none he'd call a girlfriend. Not until you."

"No, he didn't call me a girlfriend either." Rayne picked up a handful of bubbles and blew them across the tub. She imagined playing in the bath with her little girl, dark blonde curls and green laughing eyes, splashing and catching bubbles in her tiny hands.

"I'm not asking you to excuse his behavior. All I'm asking is that you give him a chance. He's been screwed up for a long time, been carrying around a boatload of hate and guilt. He needs you, Rayne. And he needs his baby."

"He can't be a father if he's not even in the same state. Trent made his decision. He finally has the career he's always dreamed of. The baby and I were never part of that dream."

After planning a lunch date for the following week, Rayne hung up, feeling confused and overwhelmed.

***

One of the benefits of owning a fitness studio was always having time to work out. Rayne didn't look twenty-four weeks pregnant. She had energy again and could still keep up with her intense Zumba class but knew in a few months, or weeks, she'd need to teach the moderate level classes. Thyme had been a godsend, filling in at the counter and teaching classes as well.

Next week would be her slowest of the year, the week between Christmas and New Year's. Too soon to worry about dieting and too busy to think about working out. The mad rush would come in January when women made their New Year's resolutions. Rayne used this time to study prenatal yoga and Pilates; she'd advertise the new offerings with her New Year specials. She proofed the ad one more time and then attached it to her email, sending it to the local newspapers.

Shutting down her laptop, she rolled her shoulders a few times and lifted her hands above her head, stretching out the kinks in her neck and shoulders.

"Long day?"

Rayne nearly fell out of her chair.

"Sorry, didn't mean to startle you." Trent

stretched his arms above his head, resting his fingertips on the molding above the door. His frame filled the doorway quite nicely, his jeans hanging low on his narrow hips, his Patriots sweatshirt rising just enough to tease her with a glimpse of his hard stomach.

"What do you want?" She didn't mean to sound so cross but she didn't like the way her body responded to him. Claire had said Trent hinted at coming home for Christmas, yet he hadn't contacted her about it. So much for him wanting to be involved. Still, he made her knees weak with lust, even if she hated how much he hurt her.

He had the audacity to smirk. "Is that the hormones talking or are you still mad at me?"

"My hormones are fine." She hoisted herself out of her chair and grabbed her winter jacket, pulling her arms through and zipping it up to her neck. "I'm on my way out. Whatever you want will have to wait."

"Where are you going?" He stayed in the doorway, blocking her exit.

"None of your business."

"Can I tag along?"

"No."

"Don't you have another doctor's appointment coming up?"

"Maybe."

"Can I come?"

"No."

Trent lowered his arms and sighed. "I'm trying, Rayne. I don't know what else to do."

"You've done enough already." She pushed past

him, trying not to notice the alluring scent of vanilla and testosterone. Unfortunately, he followed her to the parking lot.

"You can't continue to avoid me like this. I want to do the right thing here, Rayne, and you're not making it very easy. You keep pushing me away like this and maybe next time I won't come back."

She stopped in her tracks and turned to him. "That," she stabbed her finger into his chest, "is exactly why I want you to stay out of my life." Rayne got in her car, jabbed the key in the ignition, and peeled out of the parking lot.

***

Trent

"What the hell, Brian? I can't handle her hormones. Was Claire this messed up when she was pregnant?"

Trent tipped back his mug of beer and wiped his mouth on his sleeve. The New England Patriots were down by two with a minute left to go but Trent wasn't worried. He knew a perfect spiral would make it into the hands of the wide receiver and they'd win the game. Too bad he didn't have the Pats' record.

"Did she talk in rhymes and not make any sense either?"

Brian let out a grunt and grimaced. "Oh, that had to hurt. Get up, dude. There you go."

"Hey! You listening to me?" Trent punched Brian's shoulder.

"Yeah. Just a minute. Game's almost—oh, yeah! Touchdown!" Brian and the rest of the patrons in the bar let out loud cheers. How could these morons care about a stupid football game when Trent's life was going down the shitter?

Damn. The extra estrogen must be contagious. Trent was a walking Lifetime movie. He decided to let Brian come down from his Patriot-winning high before he continued with the girly talk.

They finished off their plate of potato skins, ordered another round of Bud, and haphazardly watched the start of the Jets game.

"Dude. Someone run over your puppy?" Leave it to Brian to make light of his situation.

"You didn't hear a word I said, did you?"

"I heard you pissing and moaning. Not sure how I can help you. Claire and I weren't in the same situation as you and Rayne. We actually admitted we loved each other, spoke to each other. Were married. Wanted a kid. Lived in the same time zone. Whole nine yards. You, my friend, have done none of the above."

The light bulb above Trent's head went off. "You're on to something there. Thanks, man." Trent slapped Brian's back, tossed a few bills on the table, and left. He had a plan. Finally. There'd be no way Rayne would refuse him now.

***

Trent brought Faith along when he'd asked Rayne to spend Christmas day with him but she didn't even take two seconds to think about it. She held the baby, kissed her a dozen times, nuzzled her mouth in the child's neck—oh, how he wished he was Faith—and handed her back to him and said, "I'm spending the day with my family," before closing the door in his face.

Total rejection. And he didn't give up. After eating his fill of brunch at Brian and Claire's and watching his sister open Faith's presents, he said his goodbyes and headed over to Rayne's.

Sweaty palms turned off his ignition and pocketed his keys. He looked over to the passenger seat, picked up the small package wrapped in red and silver shiny paper and let out a long sigh. Now or never.

The walk to Rayne's apartment door felt more like death row than a trip down memory lane. But this is what she wanted. He'd do anything for her. Hearing the faint sound of Christmas music and feminine laughter, he knocked lightly on the door. The conversation stopped and he soon heard footsteps approaching. Plastering on his good ol' boy charm, he leaned in as the door opened and kissed her on the lips. "Merry Christmas, beautiful."

"Merry Christmas, asswipe."

Recognizing the voice, Trent pulled back quickly. "Sage."

"Trent."

"Expecting someone else?" She smiled sweetly.

"Who is it?" Rayne asked from behind her.

"Wrong number."

Trent pushed past the domineering sister and stopped only inches from Rayne.

"What is he doing here?" she asked Sage, not

looking at him.

"Dunno. I think he was hoping to get lucky. He kissed me, but I pushed him away."

Trent rolled his eyes. "I was expecting you to open the door. Merry Christmas," he said softly.

Rayne crossed her arms in defiance, inadvertently pulling her white sweater taut over her belly. Sweat formed on his forehead and beaded above his lip. He had everything planned out on the drive over but he didn't expect her sisters to still be here. Or to feel so unwelcomed.

"Uh, can we talk?" His hands begged to reach out and touch her, feel her soft ivory skin, smell her citrus scent.

"About?" Rayne's wild, dark eyes glared at him.

Trent cleared his throat and pulled at the neck of his sweater, suddenly feeling tightness around his neck. He glanced at the drill sergeant behind him and saw Thyme peeking around the corner, a glass of wine in her hand and a soft smile on her face.

"I'd like to hear what he has to say," she said before draining her wine.

"Stay out of it, Thyme," Rayne growled.

The way he figured it, Trent had three options— a) Get Rayne alone so he could talk to her in private. Feeling the daggers in his back, he figured Sage wouldn't let that happen. b) Include all three girls in his speech, hoping young, carefree Thyme would vouch for him. c) Run like hell.

Option C sounded the best but he couldn't bail now. Feeling like a cornered, helpless puppy, he went with Option B. "Uh, can we sit down?"

Rayne didn't deny his request and didn't stop

him as he edged past her, winking at Thyme and making himself comfortable on the sofa. It was just like Rayne to put her heart into the holiday. The apartment smelled like pine and cranberry, and not an inch of surface space could be seen under the array of snowmen and Santa Claus figurines. Bright white lights twinkled from the oversized Christmas tree and a modern day singer he couldn't place sang "Rockin' Around the Christmas Tree" from the stereo. Piles of baby toys surrounded the tree. Trent gulped.

"'Kay, Grinch. Tell us why you're trying to steal our Christmas."

He felt like telling Sage she was the pot calling the kettle black, but didn't think getting into a fight with her right now would do anything for his cause. Ignoring the Ghost of Christmas Past, Trent smiled at Rayne and tapped the cushion next to him. "Will you sit, please?"

Sighing in compliance, she moved to the couch and sat as far away from him as possible. She crossed her legs, and the adorable candy cane striped socks covering her feet peeped out from under her loose pants. Would she dress their kids in matching holiday outfits every year? *Kids?* As in plural? Where the hell did that thought come from? Damaging one human being would be punishment enough. He couldn't father another.

Shaking off the thought, he brought himself back to the situation at hand. He licked his lips and opened his mouth but no words would come out. Fear trickled down his spine. Trent Kipson didn't do forever, but this wasn't about himself. He needed to get past his selfishness and do the right thing.

"Marry me," he blurted out.

Sage coughed, Thyme whistled, and Rayne didn't breathe. Okay, so not the most romantic proposal; she knew he didn't do romance. Still, he could do better. He inched closer to her on the couch and she stiffened. Trent picked up her limp hand. "We get along great. Have the same interests. Have amazing sex." Thyme giggled. That was good, right? "I don't know how to be a father or husband but I'll do whatever you need me to do. I'm taking responsibility for you and…the baby. We can make this work. You can move to California."

He covered all his bases but the room still felt frigid. Picking up the box that he set on the coffee table, he handed it to Rayne. She leaned back and crossed her arms so he opened it slowly, revealing a nice piece of bling the saleslady said would impress any woman.

"Oh my God." Thyme was impressed.

"Oh shit." Sage was not.

"What? No." Neither was Rayne. She stood up, pushing Thyme out of her way, and ran to her bedroom.

"You—" Sage kicked his shin "—are such an idiot."

Thyme shook her head in pity. "I thought you were different. I'll walk you out."

The Walk of Shame. What the hell did he do wrong? This was exactly what Rayne wanted. Commitment. The Happily Ever After. He just offered it to her and she acted like he asked her to donate both arms.

The hell with women.

***

Rayne

The New Year's Resolution Rush was exactly what Rayne needed to keep her mind off Trent's ridiculous proposal. Rayne picked up the Swiffer in the corner of the studio and wiped down the floor. Too bad she couldn't Swiffer away the pity proposal.

At least her other boyfriends had the decency to act like marrying her wasn't a life sentence. The shaky voice and sweaty palms were clearly not due to the typical proposal jitters but were from the doom that Trent felt was clouding over him…for the rest of his life. He didn't want to marry her, that was obvious. Just as obvious that he had no desire to be a father. Ever.

The last doctor's appointment went well. She started gaining some weight after a slow start, and the baby was progressing nicely. If all went according to plan—which nothing in her personal life had ever—she'd have her baby in early May. Neil and Suzie said they'd try to be back in Maine around that time but wouldn't make any promises. Story of her life. Empty promises versus no promises.

They didn't sound the least bit shocked when she called them on Thanksgiving to tell them she was pregnant.

"You always wanted kids. I'm sure you'll be a

good mom." That was the extent of Suzie's excitement and motherly advice. Not even a Christmas card for their daughters or a baby gift for their soon-to-be grandchild.

A year ago Rayne would have thought she'd be an excellent mother as well, but her personality had changed drastically over the past few months and she started to doubt herself. Was it due to pregnancy hormones or her crappy personal life?

Done for the day, Rayne shut off the stereo system, closed the blinds, and made sure the thermostat was at sixty-five. These long days were starting to take a toll on her. She found she had more energy in the afternoon and passed her morning classes to the other girls. Even the nine a.m. gentle yoga class was too much for her tired body.

Shutting the lights off, she reached in her purse for her keys and noticed a new text message on her phone.

Trent: Next time tell me when you change your appointment -T

She didn't mean to deceive him. Not completely. When Dr. Hallowell's office called to move her appointment ahead two hours she readily agreed. If she happened to forget to tell Trent about the change, well, she could blame her raging hormones. Rayne figured he'd hightailed it out on the first flight he could find back to his cushy job in the land of sin.

The doctor visits were too personal, too intimate.

She couldn't handle Trent being there physically, knowing he couldn't be there emotionally.

Ignoring the text, she zipped up her parka and headed out to her car. Her mind wandered aimlessly as she drove home. Limbs stretched, limber and exhausted, she hauled herself up her stairs, let herself into her apartment, and screamed when Sage and Thyme greeted her at the door.

"What the hell?"

"See, even her mouth has changed." Sage took Rayne's keys and purse and helped her with her coat. "Thyme, make some tea and bring some cheese and crackers in the living room when you're done."

"Why do I have to do it? How about I take Rayne and you—"

"Oh, for crying out loud. What are you two fighting about now?"

Thyme sneered at Sage and wrapped her arms around Rayne. "We're here to help you, honey."

"Your bickering isn't helping. And what is it exactly that you think you can help with?"

Sage pulled a bag of Doritos out of a grocery bag and beckoned. "Come on. Let's sit."

Doritos. Something awful happened.

"Trent? Is he okay?"

"See? Her first thought is about him. I told you."

Sage rolled her eyes. "Thyme, this isn't about you."

"Sage? What's going on?"

They sat on the couch, Rayne wedged between her sisters, the newly opened bag of Doritos in her lap. She didn't know what needed soothing, so the smell of processed cheese and spices didn't do anything for her. Yet.

"We're worried about you. You've got to cut this out." Sage held Rayne's hands as Thyme played with Rayne's ponytail.

An Intervention. They'd done the same for Thyme countless times when she'd gotten herself into trouble. Sage always the bad cop, and Rayne the good.

"Cut what out?"

"Honey, we know you care about Trent. He's a good guy." Thyme, like Rayne, tended to be blinded by good looks and charm. "His proposal may not have been uber romantic but he's trying. I think you should give him another chance."

"Hey, that's not what we agreed on." Sage swatted Thyme's hand from Rayne's hair. "Raynie." Sage turned Rayne's face toward hers. "You've changed. You're moody, you swear, you yell at Thyme and me when we fight instead of trying to solve our problems and make us kiss and make up. Girl, you've got to snap out of this funk. He's not worth it."

"Yes, he is!" Thyme turned Rayne's face. "He may not realize it yet, but he loves you. And you love him. You two are having a baby and he wants to marry you."

"No, he thinks he should marry me. It's out of obligation only. And there's no way in hell I'm moving to California."

"You're letting him ruin your life instead of moving on with it. Do you want your baby to grow up seeing his mama mopey and pissy all the time?

Besides, baker boy lives three thousand miles away. What kind of dad can he be from across the country?"

"Sage, don't be cruel. Ray-Ray." Thyme kneeled on the floor at Rayne's feet. "Follow your heart. Your head is telling you wrong things. Just like your older sister. She doesn't have a heart to listen to it, but you do. Trent's not perfect. No man is. That's your problem. You're looking for Mr. Perfect and he doesn't exist. Trent is good. And kind. And hot."

"Hey, this Intervention isn't about getting her back with Trent, it's about getting our Rayne back. I miss her."

Rayne felt like she was starring in a ping-pong match, her head ready to explode. "I need to pee." Trying to locate her ab muscles, she pushed twice before she lifted her butt off the couch. In another month she'd need a forklift.

"I appreciate what you guys are doing. And saying. I'm fine. Really."

"You're a mess, honey. Mom and Dad screwed us up and it sounds like Trent's parents did the same thing to him. You can't let that get in the way of your happiness. Take a chance."

Sage snorted. "She's taken so many chances at love in the past and look where it got her."

"Hey!" Rayne said. "I resent that. 'Tis better to have loved and lost…and all that."

"You really believe that?" Sage asked, a surprising gentleness in her voice.

"Yeah. I do. When Trent and I were happy we were…everything was so right. I want that back."

Her sisters surrounded her, wrapping their arms around Rayne. "We want that for you two, don't we, Sage?"

"Yeah, yeah. If that's what you wish. Keep the mushy stuff away from me, but you were destined for it, Raynie."

Her heart, dead, empty, and hurting just minutes ago, suddenly felt alive again.

And she really had to pee.

Chapter Fifteen

Trent

The punching bag looked like cottage cheese by the time Trent was done with it. He beat the stuffing out of one of the seams and kept hammering away until the bag fell from the hook. Using his teeth, he tore the tape off from his fists and tossed the soiled lot in the garbage.

"Rough day?"

"No more than usual." Trent grabbed a towel from his bag and wiped the sweat from his face. He pulled out a bottle of water and tossed it to Brian.

"Thanks. But I don't think I need it as much as you. My bag is still hanging." He laughed while he unscrewed the cap, took a sip, and threw it back at Trent. "Pun intended."

"Ass."

"Want to go out for a beer?"

"Not much in the mood for a bar scene. I'll drink yours if you've got any in the fridge."

Brian hesitated. "Uh, I think I'm empty. We can

go to your place."

The averted eyes and nervous tapping of his foot were Brian's tells, which made him the worst poker player on the planet. "Spill." With the market in the shitter, Trent hadn't been able to get out of the lease on his condo. Maybe it was a sign of some sort. With his new salary, he could afford keeping it and his efficiency apartment he rented in Burbank.

"Uh, uh."

"Bri," Trent warned.

"Dude. She'd kill me if—"

"What? Is it Rayne? Is she okay?" Trent grabbed Brian's drenched shirt and pulled him close.

"Dude, lay off. Rayne is fine. She, uh, went baby shopping with Claire today."

"And?"

"And they're going back to the house so Claire can give Rayne some hand-me-downs."

Trent picked up his gym bag and jogged to the locker room, Brian following at his heels. "Man, come on. Don't go over there like this. You'll scare the poor woman away. She's finally happy again, getting back to herself—" Brian stopped, realizing what he just revealed.

Trent turned on his heel and pushed Brian up against the lockers. "What the hell, man. You've seen her and haven't told me? Is this some conspiracy to keep me in the dark? You picking sides?"

"Chill, man. And…let me…go. Can't…breathe."

Dropping his forearm from Brian's neck, Trent jumped back. "Sorry." Brian leaned over, gasping for air, his purple face returning to its normal color.

"Bri."

Brian held up a hand. "Don't."

They stood in awkward silence, both breathing heavily. Trent unclenched his fists and swallowed the lump that had formed in his throat. "That was uncalled for."

"Dude."

"No, don't *Dude* me or pass this off as no big deal. I flipped. I'm sorry. None of this is your fault." He scrubbed his hands across his face and over his scalp, the hair on his head only a little longer than the scruff on his face. He had buzzed his hair before his blundering proposal to Rayne but it had already grown back.

"It's all right. If the roles were reversed, I know I'd do anything to get Claire back."

Too bad he wasn't anything like Brian. Raised in a decent family with loving parents and brothers, Brian had the life Trent had envied as a kid. Trent had never wanted to be settled down with a wife and kids like Tim the Toolman Taylor in *Home Improvement* episodes he used to watch back in elementary school. He pictured himself a Jerry Seinfeld, single until the end and very happy and successful. Although the real Seinfeld did marry. No, he pictured himself more like the show. His friends around him falling in and out of relationship crisis after crisis while he went on his merry way. Enjoying the company of a beautiful woman when the whim hit.

But Brian wasn't George or Kramer; his sister or Rayne didn't mirror Elaine in any way. So where did Trent fit in? Where would his life lead? One thing was for sure, he couldn't deal with the silence between him and Rayne. If she wouldn't marry him, at least they could be friends and raise their child in some sort of happy semblance.

"I promise not to screw anything up. I need to see her. To apologize."

"Do I dare ask what for this time?"

"Claire didn't tell you?"

Wow. The irony struck hard. Here he was, nearly choking his best friend to death because he thought he was withholding information, but it was Trent keeping Brian in the dark.

"I sort of proposed a few weeks ago."

"You what?"

"Yeah."

"Shit. I never thought I'd see the day."

"She said no."

Instead of laughing as Trent predicted, Brian reached out and squeezed Trent's shoulder. "Sorry, man. That had to…" He clicked his tongue and sighed.

"I don't know what I keep doing wrong. I brought her out to lunch after Claire set me up. I apologized and said I'd take responsibility, but she walked out on me. Then I thought it was marriage she wanted but she turned that down too."

"What is it that you want?"

"Me?"

"Yeah, you."

Trent shrugged. "Damned if I know."

"Well, then. Maybe that's the problem."

After showering and throwing on his jeans and Bruins sweatshirt, Trent waited for Brian and followed him home. He sat in the driveway for a few minutes, trying to figure out what to say. What it was that Rayne wanted? *What is it that I want?* Maybe that was the problem. Trent didn't know. He didn't have hopes and dreams like she did. A good paying job, a decent place to live, freedom. Those were important to him. He never thought much further than that.

Brian tapped on his window. "She's here," he stated the obvious, pointing to Rayne's car.

Blowing into his hands to warm them up, he walked in Brian's wake up the steps to the front door.

"Honey, I'm home," Brian shouted unnecessarily.

"Shh. You'll wake the baby. She's been up all day, playing with—oh, hey, big brother." Claire kissed Brian on the lips and Trent on the cheek, then turned back to her husband. "Explain."

"Claire," Trent interjected before Brian got in any more trouble. "I invited myself over for a beer and then he—" Rayne stepped around the corner, her arms filled with green and yellow baby blankets. "Hey, Rayne."

Claire abandoned the men and turned to Rayne. "I swear I didn't set you up. Trent invited himself over and…"

"That's okay. He belongs here more than I do."

"No," all three said at the same time. Brian cut the tension with a laugh. "You see where our loyalties lie."

"No, you shouldn't have to pick sides."

"Rayne, they don't have to pick sides. They can

be friends with you regardless of how you feel about me. This whole mess is my fault." He reached over and relieved her of the load of blankets. "There's no reason why the four of us can't hang out like a normal set of...friends."

Surprisingly, Rayne nodded. "You're right. We need to be civil around each other. For the baby's sake."

Yeah, for the baby's sake. But what about his sake? He needed her too. Part of him was envious of the protective nature she had with the baby that wasn't even born yet.

"Brian, can you help me bring up some things from the basement?" Taking the hint, he dutifully followed Claire.

Trent pulled the blankets closer to him, breathing in the familiar scent of Faith. "I remember when all she did was sleep in these blankets. Now the little squirt is crawling around, getting into all sorts of mischief." Like their child would someday.

Rayne smiled and touched the edge of the Winnie the Pooh blanket. "It's hard to believe I'll have a little one soon."

Very hard to believe.

"I should be going. I've eaten up enough of Claire's day off."

"And I'm sure she loved every minute of it." They faced each other in awkward silence using the bundle of blankets as a barrier. "I'll carry these out to the car for you."

"Thanks. We already brought a few other bags out."

Once he had the blankets loaded, he shut the

back door and shoved his hands in his pockets. "Listen. Could we go to lunch after your appointment next week?" After much begging, she'd finally sent him a list of her next few appointments and he hoped to make as many as possible.

"Aren't you going back to California?"

Hell, he hadn't thought about his job once in the past two weeks. "We start shooting in two weeks. I'll be around until then."

"Oh."

"So, your appointment? Lunch? Unless you had to change the time…" He cringed, not meaning to bring that up.

"It's still at eleven-thirty. Lunch would be nice. I'll see you then." She got in her car and drove away before he could put his foot in his mouth any further.

***

Rayne

Over the next few months, Rayne's belly grew and Trent called her every night, asking about her weight, the baby's growth, how often she got up in the night to pee. It was embarrassing, but sweet. Trent had googled pregnancy and birth and asked where Rayne fell into the statistics.

On the days she had appointments, he called her twice. Once before the appointment and again at night before she went to bed. He made her take selfies every Sunday and send them to him so he could see her belly. Again, sweet and embarrassing. They didn't talk about feelings or the future, only the present day.

Trent didn't say too much about his job. He complained about the amount of makeup and hair products they used on him and said things were going well. His pilot would air sometime in April and then he would travel the states, sampling different bakeries from Alaska to New Orleans.

They laughed often and played online games against each other, making ridiculous bets. After three months of a grueling shooting schedule, Trent flew back to Maine to be with Rayne during her final weeks of pregnancy.

She didn't trust herself to be alone with Trent but agreed to see him in the company of other people unless they were dining after a routine check-up.

The wait at the steakhouse was nearly an hour so Rayne pulled out the baby name book she carried around with her religiously.

"How about Margaret?"

"Only if she comes out eighty."

"Stop it." Rayne laughed. "It's old-fashioned but adorable. We could call her Maggie." It was only recently that Rayne changed her pronoun to *we* instead of *I*. If Trent noticed the change, he didn't comment.

"How about you pick the name if it's a girl and I pick if it's a boy?"

"That's sexist."

"Fine. We'll do it the other way. I kind of like Bertha. Sounds tough. No one would mess with a girl named Bertha."

Rayne feigned a shocked face, knowing Trent would never name his girl so rashly. "Well then, I'm rather partial to Oscar."

"The grouch?"

"Like his father."

"I'm not grouchy."

"No?"

"Only if you name my kid Oscar."

"How about Eugene?"

"Yeah, he'll never get beat up on the playground with that name."

"Okay, seriously. What do you like for names? Did you think about it when your sister was pregnant?"

"Me? I never realized parents named their babies until Claire popped her kid out and told me the baby's name. I sort of thought there was a note attached to them when the storks delivered the bundles to the front doors."

"Kipson. Party of two," the hostess called out.

Trent stood first and offered his hand. When he wasn't around, Rayne found herself wishing for that forklift. He placed his hand on the small of her back—that had gotten much larger—and escorted her through the dining room. Women turned their heads when Trent was around. He still had a GQ body while she looked like she'd swallowed a beach ball.

It simply wasn't fair. Why did the guy get to look more and more sexy and charming and so damn hot during the nine months while the woman had weight gain, water retention, stretch marks, and a leaky bladder to contend with?

"Your waitress will be right with you," the young, skinny hostess said to Trent.

"You okay, Rayne? You look like—"

"I swallowed a watermelon? No, a pumpkin. One of those giant-ass ones businesses spend hundreds of dollars on, carve out, and win all sorts of prizes for. Why don't you just paint a face on my stomach and call it a day?"

Trent looked around the restaurant and back at her again. "Did I miss something here?"

"What? You didn't see all the women gawking at you, wondering what the heck you were doing with someone like me?" All her insecurities from high school came rushing back again. She'd never lose the weight. Granted she'd only gained thirty-five pounds, but she still had ten days until her due date. And she'd never look the same again.

It took over two years to lose the last thirty pounds back in college. How could she do that now as a single mother with a new baby? Flabby skin and spare tires would not hold the interest of a virile man like Trent. A lonely tear slid down her cheek.

"Baby, what's wrong?" He shifted to her side of the table and pulled her fat body into his.

"Nothing. Hormones."

"No, I don't think so." He gently pushed her hair off her face and caught the tear on his thumb. "I'm here for you, Rayne. Whatever you need," he whispered in her ear.

Rayne turned her head and stared deep into his emerald eyes, seeing the man she fell for so many months ago. Her gaze dropped to his mouth and she licked her lips.

"You're beautiful." He placed one hand on her belly and the other behind her neck and pulled her in for a kiss. Soft and tender, just like his words. It had been too long since she felt his touch and she melted into him, clinging onto Trent for support and comfort. He tasted the same, like vanilla, and man, and forever.

"Have you had time to look at the menu?" The waitress didn't seem to care that she was interrupting a magical moment.

"Give us a few minutes," Trent said without turning to her. "I rather like what's on this menu." He returned his lips to hers and tasted and teased until the waitress came back again.

Trent shifted and ordered French onion soup and salad for her and a steak for himself before returning to his side of the bench. They stuck to the safer topics of baby names and Faith's new adventures, finishing their meal without discussing the kiss or how it would impact their future.

***

After a night of restless sleep—partially due to a Wilde thing tap dancing on her bladder and the other part due to Trent's seductive kiss—Rayne knew it was time for a change. Less than two weeks and the baby would be here. She decided to surprise Trent at Sweet Spot. He had an amazing staff and was able to keep the bakery running while in California. Smart business man, he was. Marie had taken the brunt of the responsibility and had hired another manager to help out, and from what Trent had said, business was running smoothly.

The delicious scent of vanilla and almond welcomed her as she opened the bakery doors. Funny that her senses craved the sweet smells during her pregnancy. She didn't inherit a sweet tooth but sugar cookie had become her new favorite candle to burn.

"Hi Marie. Is Trent out back?"

"Oh, you just missed him. He went to the deli on Market Street for lunch. I bet he's still there."

"Thanks. I'll try to catch him." Thankful for the warm April day and craving a thick pastrami on rye, Rayne walked the two blocks to the trendy deli. She enjoyed looking in the shop windows along the cobblestone roads of the Old Port. Spotting the deli on the other side of the road, she looked both ways for traffic and began crossing the street. She immediately noticed Trent in his bright red Red Sox shirt sitting at a table by the window.

Rayne smiled, moved her gaze to Trent's dining companion, and froze. Hurricane Katrina leaned across the table and laughed at something Trent said. They seemed cozy and perfectly matched. Her long, lean legs stretched out toward Trent, rubbing her foot against his calf.

Of course he didn't stay celibate once she became a fat cow. Men like Trent, as she was reminded of last night at the steakhouse, didn't need to do monogamous. Not that they were in a relationship. She was only having his baby, no need to stay faithful, it wasn't like they were boyfriend and girlfriend. Or engaged. Or husband and wife.

No, Trent was, and always would be, a playboy.

Rayne turned around and headed back to her car, giving him up for good.

Chapter Sixteen

Trent

Trent muttered to himself as he tossed his cell phone on the counter. Since their sweet escapade two nights ago he'd gotten no sleep and had been a grouch at the bakery when really he should be whistling a tune and turning out exemplary pastries. Instead his scones were dry, his tartlets tasteless, and fondant roses flat.

All because a lithe, sexy, dark-haired beauty didn't return his call. *Calls.* He only left one message, but she could see the four other calls he attempted. He'd hoped for a replay of the other night. Again and again. Every night. And morning sex. He'd never had morning sex. He thought about morning sex—a lot—but that would require an overnight stay.

Before the pregnancy news, he'd slept a few times at Rayne's house, slipping out before dawn, thus keeping his "no sleepover" rule in effect. If you didn't have coffee and a bagel with a woman in the morning, it simplified things.

Trent attempted to gently fold the Maine wild blueberries into his muffin mixture, when he imagined sharing one, hot from the oven and dripping with melted butter, with Rayne over a cup of steamy hazelnut blend. The picture in his head, of the two of them flushed from a night of sex, wearing whatever they could find on the floor while they ate breakfast, didn't freak him out like it had in the past.

Marie popped her head through the door that separated the kitchen from the bakery. "Trent, your client is here."

Trent eyed the clock on the wall. "Jill Henderson and her mother aren't due for another hour. I just pulled the samples out of the freezer. They won't be ready for another thirty minutes."

"It's not Miss Henderson. It's Miss Wilde."

Whipping off his apron, he nodded to the muffin batter. "Can you finish filling those and put them in the oven?" The girl in him took over, messing with his stomach, making him all gooey inside.

He pushed through the swinging doors and was instantly disappointed when he saw Sage.

"Oh, it's you."

"Well, not exactly the response I was expecting." Sage smiled coyly at him and motioned to one of the café tables. "Sit. I need to talk to you."

"Okaaay." Reluctantly he pulled out a stool for her and then sat down across from her. "What brings you by?"

"I could use my cover and tell you I'm here for business. Scouting out your bakery. Looking for new connections. With your recent fame, my clients would be lined up at your door to sample your goods." She raised her eyebrow, making her innuendo clear. "I'm not one for mind games so I'll get to the point. I love my sister. Dearly. You mess with her, I'll chop your manly parts off and slice them up in your fancy Kitchen Aid."

He didn't correct her. No point in telling her his prized, stainless steel machine didn't slice and dice, but mixed and whipped. He used it to whip up the coconut cream he used to—

"Understand?"

"What?" He clearly didn't hear her last threat.

"Don't screw with her. Rayne is sweet and trusting. If you're stringing her along, stop. Let her go. She's had enough heartache over the years. But, if you love her…"

Heat crawled up his neck and warning bells rang in his ears. "Is that all, then?" He did not plan on having this conversation with Sage Wilde. If he loved Rayne, a question he'd been churning over for the past few days, he had no intentions of sharing that with her sister. If. A big if. Trent didn't have a clue if what he felt was love or something else. "I have to get back to work." Trent pushed the swinging doors a little too harshly, causing them to crack against the wall.

"All set, Marie. I'll finish up here."

"Was that Rayne's sister? I'm sorry," Marie corrected. "That is none of my business. I didn't know if it had anything to do with Rayne's visit."

"Rayne was here? When?" The only time she had ever visited the bakery was the time she came in and seduced him. Damn, he'd die for her to do that again.

"The other day. When she met you for lunch."

"You lost me, Marie. She hasn't been here in months."

"She came by yesterday and I told her you were at the deli. She said she would walk down and catch up with you there. I figured you saw her. Oh, dear. You don't think something awful happened to her, do you? She's due to have the baby any day now."

Shit. She must have seen him having lunch with Katrina. No wonder she wouldn't answer her phone. He needed to act fast.

Only he couldn't. The Hendersons showed up for their cake testing, and then he had an onslaught of calls for summer wedding cakes. It wasn't until the end of the day that he finally had a moment to call Rayne.

As if on cue, his cell phone rang. *Rayne.* "Hi. I've been trying to reach you."

"I'm in the hospital."

"Hospital? Why? What happened?"

"I'm having my baby."

Our baby. So she was shutting him out again. "Right now?"

"Well, he didn't tell me his exact ETA but I'm—oh!" Rayne sucked in a breath, in obvious pain.

"Rayne! Talk to me!" He heard a fumbling of voices and unidentifiable noises.

"She can't talk, dumbass. She's having a contraction."

"Sage, how long has she been in labor?"

"Long enough. She was at eight centimeters the

last time the doctors checked."

"Why didn't anyone call me, damn it?" He searched through his pockets but couldn't find his keys. "Marie!"

"Breathe, Raynie, that's good. Breathe."

"Sage, let me talk to her."

"No, she needs to relax. You're not helping." Sage hung up on him.

"Marie!"

"What is it, Trent?"

"My keys, have you seen them?"

Marie pointed to the counter.

"Thanks, you're a lifesaver. Gotta go. Rayne is having our baby." He kissed Marie on the cheek and ran out the back door, nearly crashing into the dumpster. Thankfully the hospital was only a few miles away. The new security procedures held him up. He handed over his driver's license and waited impatiently for a visitor's badge. Hell, he should have been the one to bring her here, to carry her bag, to check her in. It's why the network made him work twenty-hour days, to make up for these weeks he said he needed off.

"Fourth floor, Mr. Kipson," the security receptionist hollered after him. Pushing the up arrow over and over again didn't make the elevator come any faster, but he pounded on it anyway. Tapping his foot restlessly and playing with his keys until the elevator reached the fourth floor, Trent cursed Sage for not calling him earlier. If he missed the birth of his baby there'd be hell to pay.

He read the numbers outside the doors and jogged along the corridor until he came to room

426.

"Push, honey, push!"

"No, wait!" Trent yelled as he stormed through the door.

"Trent," Rayne whispered.

"I'm here, baby." He kissed her forehead and used the washcloth by her head to wipe her damp skin.

"Trent." She squeezed her eyes shut and opened her mouth to grunt and groan as she pushed.

"That's it, Rayne. Bare down and push," the doctor encouraged from a spot between her legs.

Rayne reached out and grabbed Trent's hand, squeezing until her knuckles turned white. "You're doing great," he soothed.

"How the hell do you know? Have you ever had a baby before?" She clutched at the sheets with one hand and crushed his with the other. "Oh God!" She lifted her hand from the sheet, reached over her belly, and grabbed his belt. "Help me. Ah!" she screeched. "Get this baby out now!"

Someone made noises behind him, probably Sage, but he didn't care. All his concentration was on Rayne and their baby. "Push, honey. Push. Hold me and push."

"What does it look like I'm doing?" For the first time since he entered the room, her eyes opened. "Trent," she cooed and relaxed for a moment. "You came."

"Yeah, honey. I'm not leaving you. Hold on to me and squeeze, okay?" He dabbed her face with the cool cloth and felt her tense again.

"Oh, no. Another one."

"That's good, Rayne. One more good push and the baby's head will be out," the doctor said calmly.

Rayne grunted, and squeezed, and pushed, and minutes later the doctor held up a wet, squirmy little thing. "Congratulations. It's a boy."

"Oh, a boy," Rayne cried and held her arms out to her baby. "I have a son."

"We have a son." Trent leaned over and kissed her lips, feeling her soften beneath him. He pulled away to stare at his son. "Wow. He's…amazing." His baby's face was red and blotchy, and he remembered Faith looking the same during her first few hours. Bald as a cue ball, the little guy was perfect. And his. Pride he never thought he'd feel ran through his core, causing him to stand a little straighter; the urge to puff out his chest and claim the boy as his own ran rampant through his body. The nurse placed the naked baby on Rayne's chest and covered him with a blanket. Trent pulled the blanket back to inspect the little fingers he'd seen in the ultrasound. "Looks just like the picture."

Rayne's hands inspected the baby as well, pulling his feet out from his cocoon and rubbing her hand up and down his scrawny body.

"He has your figure."

Rayne snorted. "Hardly. Have you seen my ankles lately?"

"Unfortunately, no."

"And my stomach…oh, I can't even imagine what that looks like now."

"You're beautiful."

"As the father of my child, you're required to say that moments after I give birth."

"I don't recall reading that in those baby books." He covered their son in blankets.

"You read those?"

Trent nodded.

"Oh, gah. Get a room."

"We have one. Feel free to leave." Winking at Thyme, he ignored Sage, and returned his gaze to Rayne.

"Um, would you like to hold him?"

Trent nodded again and held the baby to his chest. Mesmerized by the tiny wonder, he couldn't imagine how any parent could abandon their child. Rayne's and his parents were terrible role models, but that didn't mean that he and Rayne would be bad parents. They could learn from their mistakes, right?

The little miracle in his arms gave him a whole new prospect in life. No job in the world, no amount of fame or money in the bank, could buy what he had right in front of him. He made this baby. He and Rayne did, and damn if he'd let anything bad ever happen to his son. Finally, after all these years, his future looked bright and clear and it didn't scare him one damn bit. He knew exactly what he wanted and had a long-term dream. Trent handed the baby back to Rayne and whispered on her lips, "Thank you," before leaving the room.

And starting his future.

***

Rayne

The air in the room shifted as soon as Trent left.

"What did he say to you?"

"Why did he leave?"

"Are you okay?"

Too many questions and not enough time to process. For a while it was like she and Trent, and then the baby, were the only ones in the room. They were a couple; him supporting her through the most important day of her life, and then the three of them together, like a family.

She didn't misread the emotion in his eyes. The experience was just as powerful for him as it was for her. So why did he walk out so abruptly without saying goodbye or explaining his sudden retreat? Her heart couldn't take the turbulence anymore. It wasn't fair to the baby or to herself.

The baby. He needed a name. She and Trent never did decide, and picking one by herself felt depressing. If he was vested in the name maybe it would help him hold an interest in their baby.

"Ray-Ray." Thyme inched closer to the bed. "Do you mind if I hold my nephew?"

"Absolutely." She handed the eight-pound, twenty-one-inch bundle to her baby sister. "He's amazing, isn't he?" His absence from her body chilled her. He'd been a part of her for nine months. It felt odd to be without him. And without Trent.

"Well, you're a bit biased, being his mama and all, but yeah, I think he's the cutest baby I've ever seen."

"And you're not biased? Hand him over to his

favorite aunt." Sage fumbled awkwardly at first but soon fit into aunty role. "Yeah, I'll have to agree with you on this one, little sis. He's the cutest. Too bad I don't know what to call him." She kissed his cheek and passed him back to Rayne.

Instantly she felt warm again, but not complete. One person was missing.

She'd managed to doze off in between the poking and prodding of the nurses and woke to her baby's tiny cry. "Hey, sweetie. Mama's right here." Rayne pulled down her drab hospital gown and nursed her son. The first few times she tried to feed him she broke into a sweat, not knowing how to hold him or how to get him to latch on. Thankfully, a lactation consultant came in and showed her how to prop pillows and cradle the baby's head.

Now they were a team. He pulled off her nipple and cooed, his tiny lips making a tiny heart shape. "Oh, how I love you."

"Knock, knock. The nurse said you were awake."

Only one voice could cause the familiar stir in her belly. "Hi."

"How's the most beautiful mother in the world doing?"

"Please," Rayne snorted. "Flattery will get you nowhere." If she only knew where he wanted to go.

He placed an enormous vase of lilies and roses on the windowsill and propped a dark brown teddy bear four times the size of the baby on a chair.

"I know." He eyed the bear and smirked. "It's pretty cliché. I couldn't help it. He's so soft."

"He'll love it. Someday."

"Can I hold him again?"

Rayne offered her son up to his father, not needing a camera to capture the image. It would stay in her memory forever. "Hey, Oscar Eugene."

Rayne snorted. "Those names are no longer on the top of my list."

"No? And such handsome names," he teased. "What's on your list?"

"What's on yours?"

"Nothing too extravagant."

"That's what I was thinking too. My sisters and I grew up being the granola girls. Thyme had it the worst. I don't want my…our son to look back and regret his name. I was thinking of…Owen," she said shyly.

"Hey, that's my middle name."

"I know." Whether Trent wanted him to be or not, Owen would always be a part of him. And her. Theirs together.

Trent nuzzled the baby's head with his cheek. "Wild Owen."

Rayne laughed. "That sure fit him in my belly but his first ten hours of life have been pretty tame. By the way, what are you doing here at two in the morning? Are you heading into the bakery soon? Or…back to California?"

"No, I'm taking the next few weeks off."

"What? You can't do that."

"It's my bakery. My job. I can do whatever I want."

"Don't you have weddings coming up? A show to shoot?"

"I'll head in to do the contracted wedding cakes.

Marie and the boys can handle the day-to-day. This—" he nuzzled the baby again "—is more important."

"Oh." Her heart swelled, but she couldn't afford to let herself fall in love again. "What about your show? I'm sure you don't have the luxury of making your own schedule just yet."

"I'll figure it out." Trent moved the giant bear aside and sat in the recliner. He leaned back, kicked his feet up on the footrest, and cradled their son to his chest. They made a beautiful image and she wished she could bottle the moment forever, but she knew Trent was not hers. It was only three days ago that he played footsies with his beautiful neighbor during lunch. And he probably had a line of women at his beck and call in LA. She was such a fool to believe he'd change his habits. A fool to believe he wasn't like the other men in her life.

Closing her eyes, she curled up in a ball and tried not to cry herself to sleep.

When she woke the sun was poking through the blinds covering the hospital windows. Only the giant bear occupied the recliner, her precious baby asleep in the bassinet next to her bed.

"Morning," a friendly nurse said as she wheeled a small cart filled with bandages, syringes, and rubber gloves. "I need to do some blood work. You feel up to that right now?"

"Do I have a choice?" Rayne grumbled as she sat up in bed.

The nurse laughed. "No, honey, you don't. I'll be quick. Promise."

True to her word, the nurse did her thing and left

the room within minutes. Rayne made her way to her private bathroom and took care of her needs. By the time she came out there were two more nurses waiting for her.

"Good morning, Ms. Wilde. We have some paperwork for you to complete while we run some tests on the baby and do his circumcision. And speaking of *the baby*, have you and the father decided on a name?"

The father. Not *her husband*, Trent would always be *the father*. Always be connected to her life in some way. No matter how angry she was with him for not reciprocating her love, she didn't want their son to feel the animosity.

"Yes. I've decided on a name."

What seemed like hours later, the nurses finally wheeled the bassinet back into her room. "He didn't feel a thing."

"Easy for you to say," Trent said as he walked in behind the nurse. "I'm so glad I don't remember this moment from my past." He placed his hand over his crotch and grimaced.

"I'll show you both how to care for him." The nurse showed Rayne and Trent how to change the tiny gauze and explained what to keep an eye on. "He'll be good as new in a few days. Little fella slept right through it."

Once they were alone again, Trent picked up his son and paced around the small room, rocking and talking to the baby. A natural. And he said he never wanted children. Rayne knew it was because he didn't trust himself, but if he could see how at ease he was with his son, the way happiness radiated through him and lit up his face every time he held the baby, Trent would surely believe in love.

Lost in a private moment between father and son, Trent smiled and laughed at his own thoughts. Caught between adoration and jealousy, Rayne scowled. Why couldn't he look at her like that? Wasn't it only seven months ago that he said he'd never have children right before accusing her of setting him up? Bitterness enveloped her. "Gavin needs me."

"Huh?" Trent looked up, as if noticing he wasn't alone in the room.

"My baby. Gavin."

"I thought we were naming him Owen."

"I changed my mind," she said defiantly, holding out her arms for *Gavin*. She knew he hated the name. Thought it sounded pretentious and artsy. Rayne didn't like the trendy name either but lied to spite Trent.

"I don't think so." He held the baby closer to his chest. "My son isn't going to be made fun of for the rest of his life."

"So you've decided to be a part of his life, then?" He stepped back as if she'd slapped him. Rayne hated the way she sounded, but Trent had yet to talk to her about his feelings and what, if any, role he'd play in little Owen's life.

"I'm trying, Rayne," he snarled between gritted teeth. "What the he—" he looked down at Owen, who seemed oblivious to the tension in the room, and whispered "—heck do you think I've been doing?"

"I wish I knew." The baby started to squirm and

Rayne's breasts instantly tightened.

"Knock, knock. I've come to check on the baby. He should be ready to eat soon." Right on cue he opened up his mouth and howled. "Oh, what a cutie." The nurse reached for the light blue bundle in Trent's arms and offered him to Rayne. "Do you remember which side you fed Owen with last?"

"My right." Balancing the baby in one arm, the nurse took one of the extra pillows from the windowsill with her free hand, propped it under Rayne's left side, and placed Owen at her chest. He rooted and found what he was searching for. The instant gratification tugged at her heart and made her love him even more.

"Well, now. It looks like you two have this down pat. Buzz if you need me." She gently patted Rayne's shoulder on her way out.

This time it was Rayne who forgot the presence of anyone else besides her and her baby. Trent's sudden movement from the corner caught her eye and she lifted her head.

"Owen, huh? What happened to Gavin?"

Rayne shrugged. "I changed my mind. The paperwork has been processed, so I guess Owen it is."

"Uh huh. What's his middle name? Or are you going to lie to me about that too?"

Guilt washed over her and she lowered her gaze to her nursing son. "I don't lie. His name is Owen Trent Kipson," she whispered.

Trent held his breath and didn't move. The room remained silent except for Owen's gentle sucking. What felt like hours, but was merely minutes later,

Trent quietly left the room, leaving Rayne once again.

Chapter Seventeen

Trent

Owen Trent Kipson. She named their son after him. Surely if she despised Trent that much she wouldn't have given their son his name. For nearly his entire life Trent had built walls around himself and lied to everyone around him, telling them he never wanted to marry, never have children, never fall in love. And he believed the lies as well.

Until he met Rayne.

And held their son.

Now the world seemed bleak and empty without them. Her sisters were with her when she left the hospital yesterday, and Claire visited Rayne and Owen this morning. The walls didn't close in around him as he'd expected while working on his new plan.

The only people he'd truly cared about before were his sister and Brian in a best friend kind of way. And Faith, but the love he felt for Owen could not compare to that for his niece. It was so much more. And what he felt for Rayne sure as hell wasn't sisterly. Not seeing her, not being with her and Owen when they left the hospital yesterday, tore him up inside, but he passed Sage in the corridor and she read him the riot act about not adding any additional stress on Rayne.

Apparently his visits were an unnecessary stress. "Screw it," he muttered to himself. He needed to see her and their baby. He grabbed his keys from the kitchen counter and headed out the door.

***

Rayne

Too tired to host any more visitors, Rayne turned off her cell phone and curled up with Owen on the couch. Examining his sweet, chubby cheeks and beautiful eyes, she saw faint glimpses of Trent. Owen definitely had his father's eyes in shape and probably color. The faint dusting of downy hair on his head was light, but that could change as well.

Owen wrapped his little fist around Rayne's index finger and fell asleep on her chest. She soon followed suit.

A while later a faint rustling in the room woke her. The warmth and slight pressure on her chest assured her the baby was still sleeping. Slowly she opened her eyes and tilted her head to her right.

"Hey. I hope I didn't wake you." Trent looked incongruous sitting on the white and blue-checkered glider. Gently rocking back and forth, he nodded to her chest. "He looks comfy."

Rayne smiled. "He's a little furnace. No need for a blanket with him near."

"So, uh, how are you feeling?"

"Okay."

"How did the bab—Owen sleep last night?"

"He didn't."

Trent shot out of the glider, startling Rayne, which in turn startled Owen, his hands flailing before he started crying. Rayne sat up and gently comforted the baby.

"Shit. I mean, crap, shoot…uh, damn, darn. I'm sorry. I didn't mean to scare him. Should we call the doctor?"

"No, he's fine." Owen stopped crying and fell back asleep the same time Trent sat next to them on the couch.

"So he's not sleeping? I thought babies slept all the time. Is something wrong?"

Rayne almost smiled at his naivety. "He was up every hour to nurse. This afternoon he's been sleeping in three-hour shifts. Hopefully I can flip-flop his schedule in the next few days. Otherwise I see a lot of late night television in my future."

"Why don't you let me help? So you can sleep."

Laughing, she gently patted Owen's back so as not to startle him. "I don't see how you can."

"Sure I can. What do you need me to do?"

"Owen needs me."

"I'm his father. He needs me too."

"You can't nurse him."

Stumped, Trent ran his hands across his face and then through his too-long-for-Trent hair. "Okay, you got me there. I can change him and rock him after so you can go back to sleep."

Rayne thought about it. "Your show—"

"Doesn't need me. I told you. I'm taking a few weeks off."

Tempted to lean on him but frightened he'd hurt her again, she shook her head. "Sage and Thyme said they'd come over at night. I'm all set. Thank you, though."

Truly irritated, Trent leaped up and paced around her small living room. "No way. Nuh-uh. You're not pushing me out of my son's life. I'm staying the night." Rayne started to protest. "And I'll be here during the day. This is what you wanted, remember? So why are you shutting me out?"

Yes, she had hoped he'd be a part of both their lives, but not because he felt guilted into it. She needed him to *want* to be there. Trent's presence would only be a reminder that she had forced him into something he didn't want. Because he was an honorable man, he'd offer child support, he'd take care of Owen's basic needs. But would he love him unconditionally? Could he love her unconditionally?

No, she didn't believe he could. This need to care for them would wear off and he'd soon return to his bachelorhood. And California.

***

Trent

Damn it to hell, that woman was stubborn. For three nights he'd stayed by her side, taking Owen from her exhausted arms as soon as she finished nursing him. Burping and changing his diapers made him actually feel closer to his son. How anyone so small could create such blowouts in his pants was beyond him, though.

During the day, Trent and Rayne took turns trying to rouse the sleeping baby. They smiled at him, brought him for walks—which instantly put him to sleep so they put off stroller time until the evening—turned up the music loud and made silly faces at him, all while Owen slept. The three-hour naps turned into four hours and the nightly feedings continued every hour.

On the fifth day they had a breakthrough. Granted, that meant little Owen was up crying all afternoon. Leaving a sleeping Rayne in her room, Trent skipped the stroller and strapped on the kangaroo-looking pouch, sweating all the while trying to put the baby in the contraption. He walked through neighborhoods, discussing mindless things with his son, all in an effort to calm the little guy.

"Come on, Little O. You gotta give your mom and me a break. I'm not getting any younger. I can't party all night like I used to. Let's just hang out for a bit, talk shop, go home and have some supper…" Trent thought of Rayne's delicious breasts that were only for Owen's taking. "You're a lucky son of a…an ass. That you are, my friend. I was a little harsh with your mom a few months ago."

Owen's cries stopped and Trent hugged his son close. "Your mom is a great person." Trent laughed. "Hell, she's awesome. Beautiful, fun, spirited, loving. She loves you, you know. You're not going to have the same childhood she did. Or I did for that matter."

He rested his hands under Owen's butt, cradling him close, and leaned down to kiss the top of his head. "I love you too, little guy. You're the best thing that ever happened to me." He kissed his son's cheek and noticed he'd fallen asleep. "Or maybe the second best. No, you and your mom are a package. The best package I've ever received."

A light bulb of an idea went off in his head. "And I know just the icing for the cake."

***

Rayne

The written instructions were vague but Rayne followed them regardless.

Trent: Meet me at my place when you both wake up.–T

It was nearly eleven by the time she'd managed to feed Owen, make breakfast, shower, feed the baby again, and do something with her face and hair. For the first time in ten days, since Owen's birth, Rayne actually made herself presentable. Trent had been a lifesaver, staying with her for a week, letting her sleep, taking care of Owen, and cleaning the apartment.

Their friendship had been renewed. While not to its original capacity, it was still better than the animosity they felt toward each other. Each day the tension lessened. And if she were to be honest with herself she'd admit the tension had been from her toward him, not the other way around.

The past few days without him had been lonely but she understood his need to get away. As he told her months ago, he never signed up for this life. His sweetness to her and Owen clutched at her heart and made her wish for things she could not have.

Slipping out of her robe, Rayne stared at her closet in resignation. Maternity clothes hung on her, but she couldn't squeeze into her jeans just yet. Pulling on a pair of worn yoga pants and a purple T-shirt, she eyed herself in the full-length mirror. Her body had definitely changed and would probably never go back to the condition it was last summer, but she didn't care anymore.

People would have to accept her as she was. No longer the insecure, overweight, reserved girl of her youth, Rayne knew she had a lot more to offer than looks. Life had taught her valuable lessons and vanity wasn't one of them. As long as she loved and respected herself, the rest would fall into place.

Dressing Owen in a Red Sox onesie and tiny dark blue pants, she talked to him and tickled his toes. "Who's the cutest baby in the world? Oh!" She thought he smiled but knew he was still too young for such tricks. Strapping him in his car seat, she kissed him once more, picked up the diaper bag, and headed out the door. "We're going to Daddy's house, pumpkin. Hopefully he'll ask us to stay. Forever."

Luckily she found a parking spot not far from Trent's brownstone. Parking in the Old Port on a beautiful day in May was a rare commodity. She unhitched the infant carrier from the back seat, pulled the diaper bag over her shoulder, and walked up the steps to Trent's house. The door opened before she could knock and Katrina, dressed in a thin silk robe, greeted her with a sneer. Trent, wearing only jeans, hair still damp from a shower or a sweaty bout of sex, stood behind her.

"Oh. It's you," Katrina snipped. "You just had a baby." She eyed Rayne up and down. "No skinny jeans for you for a while, huh?"

Neither one of them moved. Rayne couldn't make her way into Trent's house with Katrina blocking the way, and Katrina couldn't get past Rayne and the car seat on the narrow front steps.

"Katrina, let her in."

"Oh, sure, darling." Katrina backed into the house as if welcoming Rayne into *her* territory. "We're just finishing up here anyway." Katrina raked her nails down Trent's naked chest, put a key in his hand, kissed his cheek, and sauntered toward the front door. "Call me later," she called over her shoulder.

Blood that had once been circulating through her body now pooled at her feet, making them too heavy to move, and her body felt weak without it.

"Here, let me help." Trent took the infant carrier from her and set it by the couch. She held on to the diaper bag like a shield, covering the excess weight she carried. Katrina was supermodel thin and Rayne was...not. Her butt, once tight and round, sagged. Her hips, once narrow and petite, now widened from childbirth.

Of course he hadn't been celibate. It had been nearly six months since they'd had sex. Trent was a sexually active man, she couldn't expect him to wait for her, especially when he'd made it clear he had no interest in her or a relationship.

Guilt washed over his face as he attempted to take the diaper bag from her. "No, don't touch me," she said.

"Rayne, you're not going to stand there all day holding the bag. You can set it down."

"No, Owen and I are leaving. We obviously interrupted something." She reached for the handle to the carrier but he stopped her, wrapping his large hand around her wrist.

"Damn it, Rayne. Let me explain."

"No. No. You don't need to explain anything." She sniffed and turned her head. "You never said…we never…you…" A golf ball of emotion lodged in her throat, preventing any semblance of a complete thought or sentence. Unwanted tears escaped and she used her shoulder to wipe them away. Of all mornings to decide to wear mascara again.

"Sweetheart, look at me." Trent cupped her chin in his hand and turned her head. "It's not what it looks like."

Rayne laughed. "Just like your lunch, huh?"

"Yeah, actually. Will you trust me, please?" She sniffed and swiped her tears with her hand. "Please? I can explain."

"You don't owe me any explanation. You asked me to bring Owen, and I shouldn't have assumed you wanted to see me too. I'll need to come back in a couple hours to feed him."

"I wanted to see both of you. I have something to show you. I'll be right back. Don't leave. Please." He kissed her cheek before turning away toward the hall to his bedroom, leaving Rayne to her tears and woeful thoughts. She caught him with his pants down. Well, they were pulled up but not buttoned. His sculpted chest taunting her, saying, *you can look but you can't touch!* And she couldn't help but notice the way his firm, round butt filled out a pair of Levis.

Before she could change her mind, Trent came around the corner wearing a Red Sox shirt that matched Owen's. He smirked knowingly. "I bought these on the same day. Figured we'd wear them to a baseball game."

Her heart tightened. "I don't think he's old enough to appreciate a game."

"Maybe not. Better to get him accustomed to the Sox at an early age." He picked up the diaper bag and car seat.

"Where are we going?"

"It's a surprise. Trust me, okay?" He seemed vulnerable, nervous yet excited. How she could trust him after walking in on him and Katrina she didn't know, but she did. His sex life was no longer her business. Not that it ever was. He said he was faithful to the women he dated and as far as she knew, he had never turned to another woman while they were together.

So would he be faithful to Katrina as well?

They sat in silence as Trent drove south, staying close to the coast. She hoped his idea of a surprise wasn't a day on the beach. Owen's skin was too fair to be spending much time in direct sunlight and it would be years before she'd shed the forty pounds she'd gained. Standing next to thin waifs like Katrina brought her years of insecurity back.

Fifteen minutes later he wove in and out of side streets and into a gorgeous neighborhood in Rocky Harbor. He pulled into a driveway and shut off the engine. "We're here."

Trent's voice sounded shaky, unsure. He slid out of the vehicle first and unlatched the infant carrier, Owen still sound asleep. Rayne got out and followed him up the path to the house.

"Who are we visiting?"

"No one." He pulled a key out of his pocket, unlocked the door and motioned for her to go first.

The house was empty. A massive curved staircase made a bold statement in the entryway; hardwood floors gleamed throughout the living room. One large wall, painted a deep burgundy, housed a stone fireplace. Windows beckoned the warm sunlight and showed off a private wooded backyard. Rayne walked through the living room and into a state-of-the-art kitchen. Dark cherry cabinets accented by stainless steel appliances and black granite countertops.

"Wow. This is beautiful."

"I know."

She turned around to study Trent, unsure why he brought her here. His gaze fixated on her. His green irises a shade darker, similar to how they looked when they were making love.

"Rayne." He stepped closer to her and stroked

her cheek with the back of his knuckles. "God, you're beautiful."

"No, I'm frumpy and jiggly and tired. I have bags under my eyes and have—"

"The most delicious, kissable mouth. The kindest heart I've ever seen." He stepped closer, their bodies nearly touching. "An intelligent mind that keeps me on my toes. And a body that's meant for loving," he whispered into her mouth. "I want you, Rayne. I need you."

The air was warm but chills crept up her spine and tickled her belly. She craved him. But…Rayne shook her head and stepped back. "Katrina."

Trent moved closer again, invading her personal space. "Is a nosy neighbor. And my real estate agent." He picked up her hand and kissed her palm. "I had a business lunch with her a few weeks ago. I've been house shopping." He picked up her other hand and gently kissed each finger. "Searching for a family home. I thought it was you at the door this morning so I didn't think anything about not being dressed all the way. She came over to give me the key."

"Half-naked?"

"Katrina enjoys pushing the envelope. I've never, ever touched her." Trent had his faults, but he was no liar. Still, Rayne kept her guard up.

"I saw this house and thought it would be perfect. For us."

Rayne's breath caught and her eyes widened with uncertainty. "For you and Owen?"

Trent nodded. "He'll have a safe neighborhood to grow up in. A nice backyard to play in. I found an awesome spot to build a treehouse."

"Oh." No mention of her role in this move.

Smiling, Trent moved his hands to her waist and pulled her closer to him. "Wait until you see the master bedroom," he whispered in her ear.

"Oh." Maybe he did want her. But in his bed or in his life? He still hadn't said what she needed to hear.

"Come here. I have one more thing to show you." He checked on Owen, who was still sleeping in his carrier, and pulled her through the kitchen and out to the terrace. A beautiful stone patio was adorned by lilac and rose bushes and a granite bird feeder sat in the center of a garden just beginning to flourish with a multitude of flowers.

Pulling her over to a stone bench that sat nestled between a white arbor and flowering bushes, Trent gently pushed on her shoulders until she sat. He took both her hands in his and kneeled at her feet.

"Rayne," he said, kissing each palm again. "God, I've missed you. I think I've loved you since you cheated during our race at the lake."

She laughed and cried at the same time. "I didn't cheat." Her throat tightened, nervous and anxious for what he had to say next.

Trent wiped her tears away with his thumbs and kissed her lightly on the lips. "You cheated and we both know it. And I'll let you do it again in a heartbeat. I'll let you have anything you want, Rayne, as long as you agree to be my wife. I love you so much, I don't think I can go another day, hell, another hour, without you and Owen by my side."

"Trent." She sniffed and leaned in to kiss him but he pulled back.

"Wait. There are conditions."

"Your job." She pulled back as well. If he didn't love her unconditionally then there would be no marriage.

"I talked to my agent. I'll have to travel some. You and Owen can come with me when I do. I'm not going to do the show. It wasn't for me anyway. The hair, the lights, the staging aren't my style, but I'm going to do the traveling gig. My contract states I only have to do fifteen bakery visits a year. We have a pretty wide window of when to get them done, and the rest of the time we'll be home, here in Maine, or vacationing across the country. Together."

He brought her hands to his mouth and kissed her knuckles, his emerald eyes never leaving her face. "I want us to be a family. You, me, Owen, and a slew more babies. If you don't like this house we can look somewhere else. It has four bedrooms but we can add on, finish off the basement. Do whatever you'd like. I don't want to lose you, Rayne. Ever. I love you so much. And it doesn't scare me. What scares me is that I'll miss Owen's first smile. First step. That you won't be next to me each night, draped over my body every morning. Be with me forever. Do the coffee and toast thing. Please, please. Marry me."

"More babies?" There was no bead of sweat above his lip, quiver in his hands, or nervous twitch in his eye like the first time he proposed. Rayne threw herself at Trent, knocking him backward, kissing him deeply, passionately, and without any hesitation. "I have no idea what you mean about the coffee and toast thing, but I'm game. I love you, Trent Kipson. Forever. I want you. I want this house. And I want to make love to you every day and have a houseful of little Kipsons."

Their tongues mated, their bodies molded to each other's, filling each other with the love and passion they both missed and needed so much.

It was in fact, the icing on the cake.

Epilogue

Rayne

Rayne looked around her living room and smiled. This. This is what she'd dreamed of for so many years. A room full of friends and family making memories and starting traditions to pass on for generations.

Trent and Brian had finished up the Thanksgiving dishes and were arguing with Claire and Sage about the rules in charades. The men had turned down the volume of the football game and agreed to play one round if they got out of the next round of diaper duty. Faith made her way around the living room passing blocks to Owen, who sat in Thyme's lap.

Thyme had finally found her calling and had taken a job as a nanny to an adorable little five-year-old girl. Maybe now her sister would settle down and start making goals and plans for her future.

"You can't mouth the words, cheater. You're

supposed to act them out." Sage shook her head and took a sip from her wine glass.

"I didn't say anything and besides, you can't make up rules as we go." Trent crossed his arms over his chest and deferred to Rayne. "Your sister's a sore loser. Must run in the family."

"I'm not a sore loser. Sage is, though." Rayne ignored her sister's scowl and tickled Owen's feet.

"I say we put Sage and Trent on the same team," Brian suggested after pulling Claire onto his lap as a shield.

"You're just as bad," Claire said as she lightly smacked her husband's chest. "You and Trent are just trying to get out of playing so you can go back to your football game."

The game of charades had gotten a little out of control after the fourth round. They'd agreed on movie titles and the men chose movies like *Terminator, Monty Python and the Holy Grail,* and *The Hangover,* while the women put in words and phrases like *Cinderella, Pretty Woman, Bridesmaids,* and *Magic Mike.*

Of course when it was the men's turn they twisted every movie title into something erotic. Watching Brian prance around like a hooker brought them to tears and Trent twirled like he wore a princess gown, getting so dizzy that he nearly took out their wedding photo on the mantel.

Their wedding was a small and intimate backyard affair and she wouldn't trade it for anything in the world. For the longest time she'd dreamed of a big fancy wedding dress with hundreds of guests watching her walk down the aisle of a church, the long train and veil trailing behind, an elaborate white bouquet of flowers in hand. She didn't dream of the man at the altar, but the wedding itself. When Rayne finally fell in love for real, she realized it wasn't the experience but the man standing next to her, vowing to love and cherish her forever, that mattered the most.

"I think we paid our dues. How about dessert? I have a pumpkin cheesecake, lemon meringue pie, and a German chocolate cream pie," Trent said when he could finally stand up straight. "And yours will come later." He winked at Rayne before placing a kiss on her neck and whispering in her ear. "I'm going to start right here." He nibbled on her earlobe. "And work my way…very slowly…down your body, licking up every drop of blackberry sauce until you're screaming my name."

"Seriously. You two are like freaking rabbits," Sage whined before heading for the kitchen.

"I prefer the Energizer Bunny." Trent shrugged.

Rayne shivered and turned her head so she could gaze into his eyes and smiled mischievously. "I believe it's my turn to go first tonight, Kipson. And I don't plan on leaving an inch of your body untouched," she said softly.

Trent's smile matched hers as he leaned in to kiss her mouth. His lips tasted like the pumpkin cheesecake he snuck in when he thought no one was looking. He growled playfully before heading to the kitchen.

Rayne had lost the weight she'd gained while pregnant, but her body shape had changed, and she didn't mind one bit. Stretch marks and a little extra skin were worth it if she could hold and look at Owen every day for the rest of her life. Even so, she passed on dessert, still not having a sweet tooth.

Only when Trent made his blackberry vodka sauce and brought it to the bedroom. He'd whispered in her ear during dinner that he'd done just that. Brian and Claire went hand-in-hand to get their desserts as well, leaving Rayne, Thyme, and the babies alone.

"How are things going with the Davenports?" Rayne asked, picking up the rubber keys Owen dropped and handing them to Thyme.

"Awesome. Maddie is adorable. And so smart. I really like being her nanny." Thyme kissed the top of Faith's head when she offered Thyme a book. "Want a story?"

"You're a natural with kids."

"They're non-judgmental."

"Sage doesn't mean all the things she says."

Thyme shrugged and expertly lifted Faith on to the couch next to her. Rayne knew her sisters loved each other but they had an unusual way of showing it. Thyme seemed to act more frivolous around Sage just to piss her off and Sage constantly cut Thyme down for not having a solid career.

"I know, but she's kinda right. Sometimes. If you ever tell her I said that, I'll totally deny it. So, I've been thinking…maybe I can take some classes in early childhood development or education or something. I don't think I want to be a teacher. Maybe run a daycare or preschool. Kids are fun."

"And a lot of work." It would be just like Thyme to start something and not finish it. She was an excellent babysitter. However, working with children all day could be taxing. Rayne was exhausted every minute of the day and she only had one baby.

Thyme started to read the board book to Faith, but the toddler took it away after two pages and slid off the couch again. She didn't like to sit still for too long, similar to Thyme. "I have the patience for them. Probably because I'm used to dealing with Sage."

"True." Rayne laughed. "I'm proud of you. You've been a huge help to me and I know Claire and Brian have been impressed when you've watched Faith. The Davenports are as well, I'm sure."

"They're an amazing family. And so are you and Trent and Owen. I'm really proud of you, Rayne. You got what you've always dreamed of."

"I did, didn't I?" Rayne reached for Owen and cradled him to her chest. "I love my boys more than anything in the world." She'd never get tired of the smell of her baby, watching him discover something new every day. The toothless grins he greeted her with every morning. Trent had been hinting around at having another, and while she loved the idea, she wanted to wait until Owen was at least one. In the meantime, they were having fun practicing. "What is it that you dream for, Thyme?" Lost in her bliss, she nearly missed her sister's sad smile. "What's wrong?"

Thyme shrugged. "Nothing. I'm going to grab some pumpkin cheesecake before it's all gone." Thyme kissed the top of Owen's head and disappeared into the other room before Rayne could ask anything else.

Something troubled her sister. She'd gone from pure enjoyment playing with the two children to a far-off distant place. After things settled down with the holidays she'd have a heart-to-heart with her sister and help her work on her dreams as well. In the meantime, Rayne wouldn't let a moment escape her, enjoying every toothless grin and giggle of Owen's, traveling with Trent while he worked, and waking up with him every morning wrapped in his arms knowing she was truly loved.

Snuggling into her son's warmth, she kissed his chubby little cheeks and whispered in his ear, "Dreams really do come true."

The End

Acknowledgments

Each book is an adventure and would not be what it is without the support of so many people. The team at Limitless Publishing is phenomenal. Everyone from organizing to editing to cover art to marketing has been extremely supportive and encouraging. And the authors. Oh, wow. You won't find a more supportive, fun, engaging group of authors than those who write for Limitless. My heartfelt thanks to Lori Whitman for being the "it" girl. Therese Arkengerg for your superior editing, TOJ Publishing for your super cool cover design, and Lydia Blogs and team for all the marketing help. My heartfelt thanks for all you've done. Now on to book 2, Then Came You.

About The Author

Marianne Rice writes contemporary romances set in small New England towns. Her heroes are big and strong, yet value family and humor, while her heroines are smart, sexy, sometimes a little bit sassy, and are often battling a strong internal conflict. Together, they deal with real life issues and always, *always,* find everlasting love. When she's not writing, Marianne spends her time buying shoes, eating chocolate, chauffeuring her herd of children to their varying sporting events, and when there's time, cuddling with her husband, a drink in one hand, a romance book in the other.

Facebook:
http://www.facebook.com/MarianneRiceaut

Twitter:
https://twitter.com/mariannericeaut

Goodreads:
https://www.goodreads.com/MarianneRice

Website:
http://www.mariannerice.com/

Made in the USA
Charleston, SC
27 January 2016